GAMES
BILLIONAIRE

© 2024 Christine M. Walter.

All rights reserved. No part of this book may be reproduced in any form or by any means without permission in writing from the publisher, Christine Walter Publishing: email qrissyw@gmail.com. The views expressed herein are the responsibility of the author. All characters in this book are fictitious, and any resemblance to actual persons, living or dead is purely coincidental.

Edited by Alexa Martineau and Roxana Coumans

Cover artwork and interior artwork by Christine M. Walter

Book cover design by: Sapphire Midnight Designs

Book formatting design by: Christine M. Walter

GAMES OF A BILLIONAIRE

CHRISTINE M WALTER

Dedicated to
my football and gamer boys, Jared and Isaac

One

Billie

Some gamers think that it's wrong to cheat... but I think its down right left triangle up square down left square right circle cross

I always knew Ivory's wedding would be memorable, but not *this* memorable. And if someone told me that I'd be wishing to murder the groom the moment the wedding began, I'd have laughed in their face. Well, maybe I'd have been a little worried they might actually be onto something. But right now, I wanted to slap the man so hard I'd break my newly acquired nails. He didn't give me that chance. Or maybe I was too shocked, watching the groom's lily-livered backside scamper from the altar to the exit.

My attention zipped to Ivory, and upon seeing her sway, I hurried the few steps from the line of bridesmaids to her side.

"It's okay, honey. I've got you," I said, keeping her from face planting.

"Why, Billie?" Ivory asked me, her shaking hand clamping over my arm. "Why?"

"Because he's a di-ash." I typically didn't use forceful words, being raised by strict God-fearing parents and all, but I was ticked, and it didn't come out right. I mixed a few words.

The moron was standing right in front of her—he was right there looking at her smiling face—then he just walked away! *"I can't do this. I have to go"*—I call bull! Who even does that? He didn't even say sorry or give a freaking reason why!

I had known for a while that she was too good for him, but speaking up when a friend is so blissfully in love felt cruel. So, I stayed silent. Now, though, I'm regretting that decision.

Ivory lowered to the floor like a limp noodle. Her family crowded in, all talking over each other. Her mom elbowed me out of the way and fanned Ivory's face. Seeing I no longer had a place at her side to give comfort, my brain switched roles. I was out for blood. No one broke my best friend's heart.

With that thought cemented in my soul, I hurried down the aisle, kicking up rose petals with each barefoot stomp. The double doors slammed against the walls at my exit. I caught up to Shay just when he slipped into the driver's seat of his Camaro.

"Shay! You idiot!"

His eyes widened at the sight of me flying his way and he rushed to shut his door, cursing in fear. Right before I reached him the car shifted into reverse.

"That's right! You better be scared!" I dove for the hood of the car and heard a tear in my periwinkle blue chiffon gown. *Oops.* "How dare you do this to her!"

He had the sense to stop instead of driving off, but through the windshield I didn't miss his shoulders slump in defeat. "I didn't do this to hurt her. I just couldn't do it."

"And you *had* to wait when you were both standing in front of everyone, ready to say your vows! You coward!"

"Get off my car, Billie!"

"No! You get your butt back in there," I pointed to the church, "and you apologize to her and marry the most perfect girl ever in existence!"

"You don't get it!" He slammed his fist against his chest. "I don't deserve her! Everyone knows that—I've heard what they are saying about me! And it's not gonna happen! Now get off my car!"

I could see it in his eyes through the bug splattered glass. There wouldn't be a marriage today. Or ever—at least between them. I slid off. "You're right! You don't deserve her! Just run away, you coward!"

Wheels screeching, he sped out of the parking lot.

I brushed off the grime from my gown. "And wash your stupid car!" I called after him.

Forty-five minutes later I drove Ivory back to her parents' house, giving her a reprieve from the family drama Shay had started. We were both silent except for a few sniffles from her side of the car. If she wanted to talk, I'd wait for her to start.

Ivory sighed and patted my leg. "You're the best maid of honor, you know that, Billie?"

My lips pulled to one side. "Hardly, but thanks."

"No. You are. You know just what I need." She wiped the mascara mess from her eyes. "Silence to think."

"You talk when you want to, honey."

Minutes ticked by, and just as I turned left through a yellow light she called out, "Oh, no!"

Her outburst had me jerking the steering wheel, thinking some car was barreling toward us. "What?" I screeched.

"The honeymoon!"

I sighed in relief that we weren't going to die in a horrific car crash. "What about it?"

"It's a cruise," she huffed. "I've never been on a cruise."

"Then you should go."

"Alone?" She scoffed, blew her nose, then added the tissue to the growing pile at her feet. "No thanks."

"Why not? Go and get away from your family while your heart heals." She'd better. Her family was acting all crazy since the moment the turd left her at the altar.

"If I'm going then you're coming with me."

I laughed. "I can see it now … me lying on the ship's deck, dead drunk and getting sunburned. If I get any more freckles, it'll be considered tan. One giant freckle."

"I'm serious." She reached up to close the sunroof. "We could go together."

I gave her a pointed look then returned my attention to the road. "I'm not sharing a bed with you. You sleepwalk and snore."

"Do not."

"Fact. I even have Shay to back me up on that." At the mention of her now ex her face fell into agony. *I'm such a jerk.* "Sorry. I'll never mention him again."

"Yes you will. And it doesn't matter. I should have seen this coming. The truth of our relationship has been knockin' me upside the head for months now, but I was too blind to see it." She sniffed again then waved her hands as if batting flies away. "Enough of him. You paid for the trip, you should be the one to go with me. Your parents would love an excuse to watch Cas and don't tell me you have to work. You're your own boss."

I thought of all the meetings I had for work over the next week. I suppose I could push them back and take a break. Heaven knows I needed one. And Ivory needed me. But being gone from my baby girl for that long for the first time … I don't know if my mama heart could take it. Every time I thought about doing anything to cause Cassidy heartache, I worried that I would let her mother—also named Cassidy—down. I could envision her heavenly spirit bashing me over the head with her stilettos crying out, *"You promised to take care of my baby!"*

"No."

"No, what?" I asked, shooting her a glance and seeing her narrowed eyes shooting disapproval at me.

"You're not allowed to even think that you'd be letting Cassidy down. My sister chose you to adopt her daughter—you—no one else. Because she knew that you would do a fantastic job. So, stop beating yourself up for every little thing. Cassidy would agree with me about going. You need to take a break. And I need you too."

She's right. Cassidy had left a hole in both of our hearts, and I know Cassidy would want me to watch after her sister, not just her baby. Besides, baby Cas had my family. But a week away from my baby Cas would hurt my heart.

I sighed. "It's a week."

"Please." She tried to shift in her seat to face me more, but the seatbelt prevented it. "You've been saying you need to get away with adults outside of work."

True. I have mentioned it a few times.

"And you really need to date, I mean, how long has it been since you've dated? Or even kissed a guy?"

Years. Since before college, really. And my one and only kiss—if anyone would call it that—was at the age of fifteen. It wasn't so much a kiss as it was a faceplant into my lips full of braces. The idea of kissing since then has been a turn off and gave me anxiety. "How does going on a cruise with my best friend relate to dating?"

"Because I'm gonna be your wing girl and help you find a man on the cruise. Someone exotic—with an accent." She wiggled her brows. "An Italian man."

Italian. Okay. She might be on the right track. I did like pasta, so...

Ivory needed me. And maybe I needed a chance for a kiss. Get it over with, with someone I won't ever see again and won't be embarrassed if I did it horribly. I drove onto her street and sighed. "Okay, but I'm not sharing a room. I'll book my own."

She lightly slapped repeatedly at my bare shoulder. "Thank you! Thank you! This will be great! Girls' trip!"

"And I'm not flying on a commercial plane. We'll take my private jet." I grinned. "Yes. I know. I'm a spoiled brat now that I have my own. I can't go back."

"Complete brat." She grinned back.

"The brattiest."

Preston

I checked my phone for the first time since exiting the plane in Barcelona and pressed my lips into a hard line. Cassidee, drunk texting again. Not one, but sixteen texts. *Great.*

"Who's that?" Noah, my wide receiver, motioned to my phone, then moved a few steps forward in line to board the cruise ship.

"You get one guess," I grumbled.

He laughed and spoke in a high-pitched voice, "Oh Preston, I can't live without you! You rock my world, Preston. Take me back!"

I slapped the back of his head playfully. "Shut it, dope."

He shook his head. "What do you expect? You're the star player for the Arizona Nighthawks, and worth millions. Eat up the attention while you can."

Noah grabbed my arm, then immediately thought better of it and let go before my offensive lineman, Koa, could take him out. The guys—even though we liked to roughhouse—didn't want their quarterback injured. Rarely did Koa and Delany need to remind others of that fact. They took their job as linemen seriously. Delany slugged Noah's arm, probably for good measure and a gentle reminder. The people around us shuffled away, eyeing us warily. *Probably think we're a bunch of morons.*

"How long has it been since you broke up with her?" Delany pulled along his rolling luggage and we followed slowly.

"It's been almost two months. You'd think she'd figure it out by now," I answered.

"It's just like these women." Koa nudged me forward to close the space between us and the young couple ahead, hanging all over each other. "She knows you're worth millions and won't let ya go easily."

"She should have thought of that before she spent the weekend with her high school sweetheart," I said, still feeling the sting of her cheating. We hadn't dated long, and it never got serious, but I liked her and was excited to see where it went. That all came crashing down just like my first attempt at making the tallest Lego tower as a kid. Legos everywhere, leaving pain behind. Legos and feet don't get along. Neither do I and cheating exes.

"Seriously? That's what happened?" Delany asked. "Dude. That's messed up."

Noah nudged me and pointed with his chin. "You should hook up with her and take your mind off Cassidee."

I followed his line of sight to a woman sporting bright red hair with a blonde strip in her long bangs. Her curls were piled messily atop her head, with locks hanging down along the sides. Oversized sunglasses hid her eyes, and the sun glinted off a diamond stud in her nose. Short shorts and a sleeveless top showed off her long legs and curves. Her Gucci bag slid off her shoulder as she dug through it. Two years ago I could not have recognized the difference between a designer brand and something picked up at Walmart, but after dating enough Barbie doll women, I'd unwillingly learned a thing or two about fashion.

The only part of her posh appearance that was out of place was the plethora of stickers of video game logos and characters on her luggage. Also a few of Doctor Who. I raised my eyebrows. *Huh. An elegant punk nerd.* I'd be willing to bet my new sports car she was a nerdy gold digger. Something I didn't need.

"I'm not lookin' to hook up. I'm here because y'all made me come."

"The woman with her ain't bad either." Delany watched the two with quick, covert glances.

The woman beside the redhead had jet-black hair and beautiful dark skin. She, too, had a certain grace about her, but no evidence of a gamer presence. I jerked my head away seconds after the redhead turned my way. Had she caught me looking? The last thing I wanted was to give the impression I was interested.

I unzipped my backpack to find my passport when I felt something tap my shoe. Some kind of makeup container resting against my sneakers.

"I am so sorry. It got away from me." The redhead bent beside me to pick the item up before I could reach it. That's when I caught the scent of berries, perhaps from her shampoo. Not what I expected. I thought she'd smell like expensive perfume. She stood and held up the item like it was a trophy. "Got it. Sorry for disturbing you." Large, makeup-free azure eyes locked with mine. Beautiful. Why on earth did this stunning woman have makeup in her bag? She didn't need it. Her freckled skin looked great without it.

"Hey, Preston!" someone to my right called. Stupidly, I turned and fell into a paparazzi's trap. The guy's face hid behind a large camera, but there was no mistaking his target.

The redhead swore and hastily made an exit back to where her friend stood waiting to board. And of course, Noah posed for the photos like the ham he is. Within seconds, a cruise line employee rushed in and dragged the guy away. I just hoped word wouldn't get out about our location—this was not how I wanted to kick off my vacation.

The woman reached the entrance to the ship before we did. She handed her boarding pass to the man dressed in uniform. Seconds later she disappeared into the crowd. Not that I was paying any attention to her whereabouts like I was drawn to her. I wasn't.

The three groups in front of us took their time, but we eventually got through and headed inside. I'd been on cruises before, so seeing the large rooms with glass elevators and huge pieces of artistic centerpiece fountains wasn't new. My friends and I parted ways to find our rooms. When I reached my cabin door, I found the redhead and her friend standing outside a door next to my own. The redhead seemed to be consoling the other woman and discussing switching rooms.

Whatever was going on, I didn't want to get in the middle of female emotions, so I rushed into my room and shut the door.

Alone, at last.

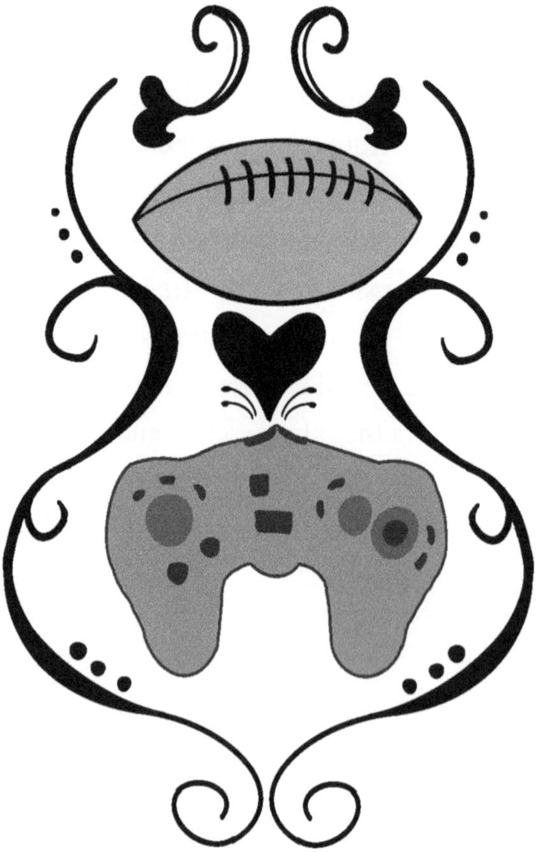

Two

Billie

A nervous first-time cruiser asked the Captain, "Do ships like this sink very often?" No, replied the Captain, "Usually only once."

Perfect. Juuust perfect. Even after my assistant called to warn the employees and change the accommodation for Ivory's cabin, they still messed it up. After Shay left her at the altar I made changes to the cruise tickets.

"Billie, please trade with me." Ivory wiped at the tears in her eyes as she glanced over the room, not stepping a foot inside.

"But this room has the balcony. You'll want the balcony." I argued.

"But I don't want to be reminded every dang day that this was supposed to be a honeymoon. Look at it!" She pointed in the room at the swan towels and rose petals on the bed. "It looks like valentines blew up in here."

"It kinda does, doesn't it?"

"Hang on." Ivory stepped in the room and picked up the chilled bottle of champagne. "I'll take this. You get this room, and I'll take yours. Aint no way I'm gonna deal with all this."

"Fine." I pulled my suitcase into the room and parked it on the bed. Did I need the reminder that I didn't have a man on my arm either? No. But I'd suck it up and take one for the team.

"Come on, Billie. Let's go find my room." Ivory dragged her suitcase out the door and I followed. I brushed my curly mess from out of my eyes and hurried down the hall. Her room ended up being one floor down, almost directly below my own. Thankfully, it was free of roses and heart shaped swans.

"I'm really sorry about all of that." I was even more sorry that she was dumped on her wedding day. I sat on her bed and watched her unpack her stuff into the tiny closet and drawers. "Candace told me that she called and had them change it so your package was no longer a honeymoon cruise. Maybe I'll talk to someone at the desk and figure it out."

"Don't worry about it. I'm just glad you're here with me. It's been far too long since I've spent time face to face with my BFF." She pulled me into a hug. She really was my BFF. My only F come to think of it. Back when I turned twenty-five and went from a struggling writer and gaming geek to earning my first million, I'd lost everyone. Either my friends thought I was too good for them, or they all seemed to want to use me for my money. That didn't sit too well with me. Even my family members acted strange. Only my immediate family, Cassidy, and Ivory stood by my side and treated me the same. After suddenly losing Cassidy, Ivory stepped in to keep me grounded and didn't let my head get too giant. So, buying her a honeymoon cruise with all the bonus excursions was a no-brainer. My gift to her after all she'd done for me. But I'd always be in debt.

"You know, I think we both need this vacay. Now that my latest game is out, I can take a break and relax," I said, rubbing my hand along the soft bedding.

Ivory opened her drawer where she'd shoved her clothing.

"Then get your skinny white butt in a swimsuit and let's go check out the pool."

"Right." I huffed. "Skinny. I've got some junk in my trunk."

She laughed. "Just enough to get the guys' heads turning. Did you notice the group in line behind us when we were boarding? Those were some nice hunks of flesh."

Hearing her talk about guys made me feel a bit better. Maybe she'd be okay and not pine over her ex for too long. He wasn't worth it. "They did look cute. If you're into the large-linebacker-break-your-bones-just-by-looking-at-you kinda guy." I stood from the bed. "I'll meet you at the elevator and we'll go to the pool together," I said, then hurried back up to my room. I took a few minutes to remove the petals and fluff from the room, dropping it out into the hall. I notified the front desk of the mix up and asked someone to remove said "fluff."

I changed into my two-piece and lace cover up and headed down the hall with my laptop bag in hand. The arrow indicating its arrival took its sweet time lighting up. When it finally dinged, I rushed in without checking to see if the elevator was empty, my mind still focused on work. I stopped abruptly against a solid chest, stumbled back, and peeked up into a surprised face. The man's mocha eyes assessed me, taking me in from head to toe. The same eyes that I had the privilege of noticing earlier in the boarding line when my makeup grew legs and ran away.

"Sorry." I stepped aside and let him out. "My bad."

He didn't respond as he walked out. He watched me until the doors closed. What a weirdo. A cute weirdo, but a weirdo just the same.

Ivory and I arrived at the poolside a few minutes later. She kicked off her sandals and pointed at my bag. "You're not planning on working the whole time, are you?"

"Psstchah. No. It's not work when you're having fun. Besides, I paid extra for the satellite connection so I can't let that go to waste." I sat in a lounge chair under the shade and placed the laptop between my legs.

"Well, while you're havin' *fun* I'm gonna *relax* in the hot tub. You'd better join me at some point or I'm asking for somethin' else for a weddin' gift."

"I'll be there in a minute. I have to check my emails and see if I can talk to Cas."

"It's the middle of the night back home. You'll have to wait until around dinner time."

"Oh, yeah." I logged onto the wi-fi and opened my inbox. From the corner of my eye, I saw Ivory lower herself into the hot tub.

An email from Chaz indicated an issue with the new game I'd developed for my newest line of game consoles. Going up against the biggest game consoles in the world was a bit daunting at first, but things took off simply because my games were different from any other out there. Each game character had a backstory and their own set of books to go with it. During the last three Black Friday doorbuster sales, people had fistfights just to get the games I'd developed and the books. My gaming company exploded faster than I ever expected.

My adolescent dreams and all my work had paid off, thanks to my team that stuck by my side.

I gave Chaz a quick call and left a message for him to call me back. Then I felt stupid, realizing the nine-hour time difference between Arizona and Spain.

Out of the corner of my eye, I saw a group of three men joining Ivory in the hot tub. A conversation I could barely hear started up between Ivory and the men. I knew any second she'd call for me to join her. Sure enough…

"Billie. Get your butt over here."

"Coming." She needed her wing girl. I slipped my laptop into the bag and walked to the spa. All eyes were on me as I lowered into the hot tub. *Great. Just what I needed. An audience.* "Hey howdy hey." I waved at the men.

Each one of them smiled and said hello.

"It's a small world." Ivory waved at a blond man wearing swim trunks and a grin. "This guy is from Texas."

"No kidding." My smile grew bigger and recognized the group as the big brutes from earlier. "Where from?"

"Dallas," he answered, then added, "Preston—our other friend—is from Dallas, too. These two schmucks," he gestured to his friends, "are from Oklahoma. But we all live in Arizona now." They kept casting glances as if they were amused at something.

"That's crazy! We live in Arizona and I'm from Texas too—well, sort of," I said. "I grew up all over, but mostly Texas."

"All over is a lot of places," the man with the man bun said.

I shrugged. "I was a military brat until my dad settled down to teach school." Hopefully, that was enough of an explanation.

My eyes were drawn to a man walking our way. The same man I ran into at the elevator and I accosted with my makeup. He had longish hair with the sides pulled back, and the scruff on his face made him look handsome and rugged in a primitive hunter-gatherer kind of way. He lowered himself in the spa and nudged one of the guys to make room for him.

"Hey, Kyler, these lovely ladies are from Texas and currently live in Arizona too," another of them said to the newcomer.

"Get out! What a small world." He smiled and nodded at us. "My name is Preston Kyler." he held his hand out to me since I sat closest.

I shook his hand and found myself reacting internally, like my heart noticed and wanted to say something important. The space in my ribs grew, pounding enough that my breath caught. "Billie," I whispered.

"Your name is Billie?" the other long-haired guy asked me, leaning in.

"Yep. I have three brothers, and I guess my parents didn't know how to name a girl."

They laughed and continued the introductions. The guy with blond hair was Noah MacClery. Then there was the Polynesian guy named Koa Kahale, and a dark-skinned, quiet guy named Trevon Delany.

"Your names sound familiar," Ivory said to Preston then pointed at Trevon. "Mostly yours."

Preston

And here it comes. Any second now the recognition and the fawning would begin. Same with every girl we met.

"You watch football?" Koa asked as I expected he would.

Ivory's eyes widened at me. "You're the quarterback for the Arizona Nighthawks."

I smiled politely. "Yes, ma'am." Not wanting to be the center of attention, I gestured to my buddies and called them out. "We all play for the Nighthawks."

"No way! That's crazy. And y'all decided that a cruise was in order now that it's off season?" Ivory asked. "That's crazy! You guys did pretty great this season…"

I twisted to Billie, noticing she stayed quiet while Ivory started chatting with my buddies. I opened my mouth to speak, but she beat me to it.

"Sorry. I'm not a football fan so I have no idea who you are. I'm pretty sure that when my brothers find out I met y'all, they'll tease me until the cows come home and then some. I'll never hear the end of it."

"That's okay. I don't expect everyone to be a fan." In fact, I kind of liked that she didn't know me from Adam.

"What are you two doing on the cruise?" Noah asked.

The women shared a look and I didn't miss the sadness in their eyes. Ivory gave a slight shake of her head then Billie spoke up. "We're just having a girls' getaway. Getting away from work for a while."

"Well, *some* of us will stop working." Ivory's accusing tone spoke volumes that she wasn't happy with her friend.

"What? I have things I need to take care of," Billie said with a hint of sass.

"What do you do for work?" I asked Billie.

Her smile faltered.

"She a—"

"Hush! Don't you dare!" Billie interrupted Ivory.

"What? Brag a little, girl." Ivory winked at her.

Noah chimed in and, of course, said something stupid. "What? Are you a stripper or something?"

Billie's face flamed as red as her hair.

Ivory threw back her head and laughed. "Heck no! Billie's as pure as one can get. You should see how embarrassed she gets when watching a rated R movie."

"Ivory! Shut up!" Billie growled. Ivory yelped as though Billie pinched her. Billie gave a wan smile and a nervous giggle. "My parents raised us with certain morals."

I leaned in and whispered, "That's commendable."

She gave me a nervous laugh and lowered herself up to her neck in the water.

"Is your job embarrassing?" I asked.

"No. Just people tend to put me into a box I don't want to be in when they find out what I do," she answered.

"I can understand that," I said. "It's kind of the same for me."

"Well, not that it matters but I could tell y'all are football players just by the size of your necks," Ivory added.

A nearby phone rang out and I recognized the *Immigrant Song* by Led Zeppelin.

Billie shot out of the water and hurried to a chair where she pulled a phone out of the pocket of a bag. I half-listened to the conversation between Ivory and the guys and kept my eye on Billie. Dang, she was hot. The freckles covering her body were adorable.

She returned with the phone still to her ear. "Ivory. I'm gonna go to the game room and figure out an issue. My laptop isn't charged enough to get it done here."

"You're ditchin' me?" Ivory frowned.

"We'll hang with ya," Delany said with a smile. "And when we're done here, we'll join Billie in the game room."

"I didn't even know they had a game room here," Ivory added.

"Why do you think I was so excited to bring my stuff?" Billie asked with a grin. "I'll see you soon. I'm gonna go shower first."

"Meet you there then," Ivory said then turned back to us.

"See y'all later." Billie waved and was off.

"So, what does she do?" Noah asked once she was out of sight.

"She doesn't like people to know." Ivory leaned in, ready to share a secret. "So, I'll just share enough. She's a gamer."

Noah's grin grew. "Like a nerd in the basement of her parents' house, kind of gamer?"

Ivory half shrugged. "Sort of."

"Does she live with her parents?" Koa asked.

"Yes," she answered as if she wasn't sure. "But she's successful at what she does."

"She's probably a virgin. Am I right?" If I could have reached Noah, I would have slugged him for asking such a stupid question.

Ivory pressed her lips together, but her look said it all.

"She *is* a virgin!" Noah laughed. "She's like a freakin' unicorn."

"Shut up, Noah." I needed to change the subject. "What do you do?"

Ivory wiggled her fingers on her right hand, full of rings. "I make jewelry and sell it on Etsy."

"Do you sell enough to make it worth it?"

She shrugged. "It pays the bills."

"Do either of you have a boyfriend?" Koa asked, which shocked me. Had I been standing I would have fallen over. I'd never heard Koa be so bold and ask a girl about her dating life.

"No," her answer was short and her tone soft.

"I sense some story there," Noah said and I gave him a death look warning him to shut up. He ignored me.

Ivory sighed. "This was supposed to be my honeymoon, but that didn't pan out. The S.O.B. is no longer in the picture and I'm single."

"I'm sorry," Koa and I said in unison.

"It's fine." She smiled, though it didn't reach her eyes. "Billie talked me into going on the cruise anyway and having some fun to forget about him."

"We can help you have some fun," Noah said, giving his winning smile.

"Oh, brother," I said and splashed him. "You're the last person she wants showing her a fun time."

"Oh, I don't know. Y'all seem nice to me. I'm sure we could think of something fun," she said.

After another thirty minutes of talking and some of us flirting we all dispersed back to our own rooms with the promise to meet in the main hall. With new cologne and clean clothes, I hurried down to the meeting spot. I was the last to arrive, so we headed to the gaming room right away. When we entered my jaw dropped. Six large screens were hung around the room. Down the middle stood a few tall tables with stools. At one end was a bar that was currently void of bartenders. Each screen was surrounded by large bean bags and gaming chairs. A couple of teens sat at one screen, silently playing a racing game. Billie sat in another bean bag with a controller in hand. What captured my attention was her long, wildly curly hair hanging down her back. The second thing I noticed was a video game I'd only seen trailers for. It hadn't even come out yet—in fact, it was months away.

"How in the world did you get this game?" I asked.

"Is that Scant Two?" Koa asked and sat down in a chair close to Billie.

"Yep." She held a phone up to her ear and spoke into it. "Now where exactly?"

I lowered myself onto the edge of the bean bag she sat in. She shifted to give me room.

"Oh, wait," Billie moved her game character around a barrel. The game glitched and the character seemed to enter a void of black then twitched. The limbs of the character jerked about unnaturally. "I found it. That is hilarious! Yeah, go ahead and fix that," she said and paused, "No. You've got the smarts to fix it. You don't need me." A pause. "Kay. Let me know if you need anything. See ya." She let the phone drop into her lap as she hit the buttons on the controller.

"How did you get your hands on that game? It's not gonna be out for months," I said in awe.

"I have sources." She grinned and winked at me.

"I'd love to know your sources," I said at the same time Koa asked if she'd played it all the way through yet.

"I have played it. Would you like to see?" she asked.

"Yes!" Both Koa and I spoke together like two twelve-year-olds. All we needed was our voices to break and a few pimples and we'd be set.

"Hey, do you know when the bar opens?" Noah asked.

"Not until nine-thirty." Ivory pointed at a sign on the bar.

The game reloaded and Billie handed the controller over to me. "Give it a whirl."

"Seriously?" *Was this Christmas?* "I've been waiting for this game since I beat the first one."

"Well, as you saw it has some glitches. But it's still in the works, so it's to be expected."

"Do you work at Legions Gaming?" Koa asked.

"Yep," she said beside me, but in her tone, I could hear there was something she wasn't saying.

"Why were you embarrassed about that?" I asked.

"I get labeled as a nerd," she said then pointed to the screen. "See that map on the side? Click the right upper trigger and it opens." She touched my finger where it was located and I felt a zing jumpstart my nervous system.

"And you can go anywhere?" I asked.

"Yep. There's no limit to where you can go." She twisted to watch me.

The game was much like the previous game, but with better graphics and easier maneuvering. I played until my leg grew dead from how many times Koa slugged it asking for a turn. I handed the controller over to him, then turned to Billie. "So, what do you do at Legion?"

"A little of everything."

"Do you know when the books come out for this game?" With all the other games from Legion Gaming there were always books to go along with the story plot of the game. The writer, known as B. A. Leigh had made millions just by the sale of his books. It was part of the draw to have the books come out around the same time as the game, and I couldn't wait to get my hands on them.

"The same week as the game." She stood and held up her phone. "I need to make a call. I'll be back in a minute."

As excited as I was about getting early access to the game, my gaze drifted over and over to the corner of the room where Billie typed away on her laptop. Her lips moved as she spoke into a Bluetooth earpiece. Every once in a while she would pull her hair back or flip it to the side, looking a bit flustered. A few times she wiggled her nose as if she were used to glasses resting there.

Noah nudged me. "I can tell you're interested. Go ask her out, man."

I gave him a look of annoyance. "Not interested in someone out for money."

"What makes you think she's out for money?" he asked.

"Every woman I've met that has designer things—you know what? I just know. I don't need to explain."

"Does it matter? Have a fling for the week. I know you're into redheads. Enjoy your time with her."

"No thanks."

He leaned closer, lowering his voice. "She's hot."

"I admit she is, but I'm not interested."

"Then maybe I am." His brows lifted briefly.

Something in his tone, or his words, or his face—don't know what—made me want to sock him in the nose. But he was one of my best friends. Why would I care if he went for a girl I thought was off the charts good looking?

Games of a Billionaire

What did I care?

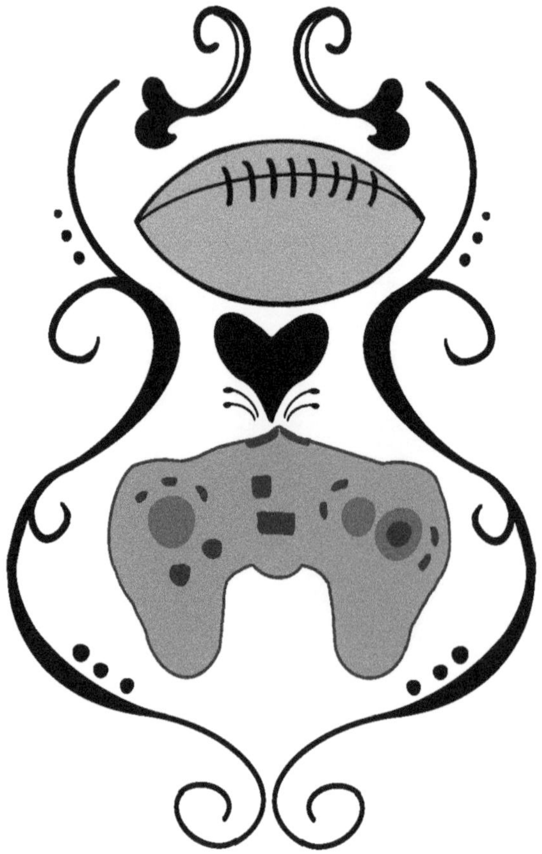

Three

Billie

A gamer buys a PlayStation and starts an EA game...
Pay just $9.99 to unlock this joke!

I stared at my plate and cringed. The food held no appeal. Not after tossing my cookies into the toilet the night before. "I swear, if these motion sickness pills don't do their job, I'm gonna kill someone," I said. Then to not sound so psychotic, I added, "Or seriously maim someone."

"It will be okay. This is the only full day of sea travel. The rest of the time we'll travel during the night, so you'll be sleeping through it anyway," Ivory said and took a bite of her bacon.

I watched her, envying her ability to eat bacon. *Oh, bacon. How I once loved thee*. But my stomach had gone on a revolt and disowned me.

All I could do to not think of the oatmeal and eggs in front of me was watch the people around the room. For whatever reason, we'd been given our own table we didn't have to share. It might have been due to the Honeymoon Special I'd purchased. I didn't know, but right now I was glad.

At least I was for a moment.

Four bodies soon joined us at our circular booth.

"Hey, Ivory. Hey, Billie," Noah said as he slid into the seat beside me. He gave me a once over. "You don't look so good." The other guys all sat around the table and greeted us as well.

"Awe, shucks. Such flattery," I grumbled.

"She's got motion sickness." Ivory pointed her fork at me.

"Oh, sorry. I guess I should have kept my mouth shut," Noah said with a repentant look.

I patted his knee briefly. "It's okay. I'll be fine soon. I took some pills." I dropped my head against my arms on the table and groaned.

"It might help if you sleep it off until the pills kick in," Preston said as he watched me with furrowed brows. "Do you need help?"

Awe. He cared. How nice. I smiled, though he didn't see since my head was buried.

"Hopefully you'll feel better tomorrow," Noah stated. "Do you have an excursion planned for tomorrow?"

"Yeah. We're going on a tour of some old Roman ruins in Tunis," Ivory answered for us.

"I'll be better by then," I mumbled from the tabletop.

I heard Koa call for a waiter. "Excuse me. Can you bring her some chamomile tea?"

"Right away," the waiter responded.

When I lifted my head in question, Koa explained. "It will help with motion sickness."

"Oh, bless your little pink bottom," I said to him which caused a bit of chuckles around the table.

Koa reached from the other side of the table for my hand. "There's also a pressure point on your wrist that will help." He touched the spot and rubbed.

"How do you know this?" I asked.

"My mom is a wise woman," he answered.

"Koa is a mama's boy," Noah said.

"And it sounds like he has a good reason. She must be awesome," I said and smiled at Koa.

"His mama is pretty awesome," Preston said, his attention fixed on Koa rubbing my wrist.

"Do you have an awesome mama, too?" I asked Preston.

He nodded. "She's pretty cool. We have our moments, but she's a good mom."

I made the mistake of looking down at my plate. I cussed and stood on the bench so I could step over Noah instead of waiting for him to move. "I need the bathroom." I ran in the direction of the lady's room.

Once I was through emptying my insides, I exited the bathroom to find Preston waiting by the door. He looked me over then asked, "Are you feeling better?"

"Only a bit."

He held up a foam cup of tea. "We got your tea to go. I'll walk you back to your room if you want help."

I took his arm and leaned against him. "Thank you. You're so nice to do that."

"It's no problem."

"I hope you don't mind that I lean my sweaty self on you."

"That's what I'm here for," he said and walked along with me to the elevator. As we stood in the moving box that didn't make things better, he held out the tea for me. "You wanna try some?"

I smiled at him and took the tea. "Thanks." *O. M. G. He's so nice. And so handsome.* The one sip didn't do much, so I held onto it and his arm as we continued on to my room. When he reached my door he helped me unlock it and guided me to the bed where he pulled the covers down. His fingers brushed my hair back from my face after he tucked me in. He even put my tea on the nightstand and turned off the light.

"Rest well," he said as he backed up toward the door.

"Thank you, Preston."

"Anytime," he whispered, then the door clicked shut. Not only did he support me physically, but his actions also provided a mental distraction from my illness. I stopped focusing on my stomach and instead became aware of how the skin on my cheek felt. His touch still lingered, and my heart raced. An image flashed in my mind of him holding me close and gently brushing his fingers against my cheek. Why? I hardly knew him, but I couldn't help wondering what it would be like to know him better.

Preston

A shove into my shoulder nearly caused me to run into a potted tree sitting in the corner by the elevator. I shoved Koa back. He laughed and shook his head. "You don't want to be playing this game, man."

He was right. He had fifty pounds on me and everyone knew you don't mess with a defensive end. Especially Koa. I held up my hands. "You started it."

"Careful with our quarterback, Koa. We need him to kick trash this next season," Delany stated then paused, taking note of three women walking around the corner.

"O.M.G! You're Preston Kyler!" The woman with dark brown hair pointed at me, bouncing on her toes. She pulled her designer bag up her arm then pointed to Noah. "And you're Noah MacClery!"

"Hi." I shook her hand and noticed how long her red nails were. How did anyone do anything with nails sticking out an inch long?

They were even longer than her obviously fake lashes.

"I'm Josie." She pointed at a blonde beside her and a strawberry blonde at her other side, "And this is Mallory and Trisha. Everyone in my family is a huge fan of the Nighthawks."

Noah shook her hand. "These guys are on the team as well. This is Trevon Delany, but we just call him Delany. And this is Koa Kahale."

"Most people don't know us. Our positions aren't as popular as quarterbacks and receivers." Delany bumped his shoulder against mine. I grinned at him, just to rub it in.

"Yeah, but we're much better lookin'," Koa said then laughed when Noah pushed him.

"Are you ladies going to dinner?" Noah asked.

"We are, yes," Trisha answered then moved closer to Noah.

"Would you like to join us?" Noah asked.

I nudged him. "Ivory and Billie are meeting us, remember?"

"Oh, they can join us too," Josie said with a smile at me. She tossed her stick straight dark hair over her shoulder and fell into step beside me as we all made our way into the dining hall. We had assigned tables, but when we asked to make different arrangements, we were able to get two tables together, one of which was Ivory and Billie's table. The two ladies were already at the table waiting for us.

I wanted to sit beside Billie and ask how she felt, so I hurried to her side of the bench. Josie followed me, even though there wasn't enough space right next to me. She quickly took the chair and set it as close as she could next to me.

Billie and Ivory both looked like deer caught in headlights when we arrived with more than they bargained for. I waved at them. "This is Josie and her two friends…"

"Trisha and Mallory," Josie supplied.

"This is Billie and Ivory," I said, gesturing to them.

"Oh, I thought Billie would have been another teammate." Josie couldn't hide her disappointment as she cast a glance at Billie.

"Yeah, I get mistaken for a football player all the time," Billie responded with a flex of her arms.

I tried to hide my laugh with a cough. "You look like you're feeling better."

"I am. Thanks for your help earlier," Billie said with a smile that lit up her eyes.

"Anytime."

"So, tell me, Preston Kyler." Josie placed a hand on my arm, almost possessively. "How much longer do you plan to play for the NFL?"

"Until I can't," I answered and wondered why she giggled and thought it was funny.

Ivory fell into conversation with Koa, while Josie dominated my attention by her excessive flirting and questions. Josie's two friends sat at the next table with Delany and Noah and sounded as though they were having a lively conversation. I kept trying to turn to Billie and include her, but Josie didn't allow it with her tugging on my arm to get my attention.

When our meals were finished, we all stood and walked out of the dining hall. Ivory spoke loud enough for everyone to hear, "We should meet at the club for drinks later."

"I would love that!" Josie said and took my arm. "Will you dance with me?"

"Sure," I said, not because I wanted to, but because my mama would thump me on the head if I were rude to a lady.

Billie took Ivory's arm and tugged her away. "We'll see y'all there."

"See ya." I waved at her, feeling like a jerk for having inadvertently ignored her during dinner. Part of me wished to keep to my room and not go to the club. Why would I want to mingle with more money-grubbing women like my ex, Cassidee?

Billie

I opened the door to my cabin and took in Ivory's smokin' hot cocktail dress with a bit of envy. I could never feel comfortable in something so form fitting. "You look hot."

She waved at my jeans and blouse. "You're going to change, right?"

I gestured at myself. "What's wrong with this?"

She rolled her eyes. "Let me see your clothes."

I sighed and let her into my room. "You always do this."

"Because I have to. You're fashionably challenged." She opened the closet and shuffled through my three maxi dresses. "You know you need to buy something more suitable for posh parties."

"Posh? Did you just say posh?"

"Yeah." She pulled out the spaghetti strap dress and held it out. "I've been watching the BBC a lot lately. I think I'm going Brit."

"I forget you're as much of a nerd as I am."

"I'm a book nerd. You're a gamer nerd. There's a difference."

I sighed. "I know I need a wardrobe change now that I'm being invited to all the fundraisers, black tie events, and galas, but can't a girl just live in jeans and a t-shirt?"

"Girl, you're almost a billionaire, so it comes with the territory. Get used to it." She hung the dress back up. "There are a few shops downstairs. We should go find you something. It won't take long."

Reluctantly, I followed her out of the room with my purse in hand. Shopping with Ivory was always an adventure, but I never walked away empty-handed. Nor did I walk away without my abs sore from laughter. She was a balm to my soul, and I was glad to be here with her so she wouldn't wallow in her heartache.

Ivory found me four cocktail dresses that made me feel like a million bucks. I had to hand it to her. She knew her stuff. The dresses weren't my style, but I bought them anyway. Once we were back in my room I changed into a strapless dress with a plunging neckline. What I loved most about it was the built-in bra padding and how the flowing chiffon brushed against my knees. The peacock green complemented my skin and hair and caused my eyes to pop.

When Ivory finished zipping me up she twirled her finger around, wanting me to spin. "Oh, my lanta. The boys are gonna drool all over you tonight, honey. Especially, if they knew how much you were worth."

"And you're *not* gonna tell them." I scowled at her then grabbed my clutch to add my card key and phone into it.

"Why would I do that? I know your rules and I haven't forgotten what happened last time someone found out how much you made."

I shivered, remembering how the guy stalked me for months until I finally had to move. He wasn't the only one that chased me, but he was the most persistent. I needed to move anyway, so he really was doing me a favor in the end.

Ivory opened her wristlet and frowned. "I forgot my lip gloss. I'm gonna go down and get it and I'll meet you at the club."

"Okay, see you there," I said, stepping into the bathroom so I could add a touch of red to my lips. I brushed my fingers through my hair that hung to my elbows and decided I looked pretty good. As I stepped out of my room, I heard the door next to mine close. I turned just as Preston did. We stood there for a moment, both checking each other out. Whoever designed his buttoned shirt and slacks must have had him in mind. The Animaniacs calling out *hello nurse!* came to mind, but of course it would be *hello, handsome!* He wasn't a nurse after all.

"Hi—uh, hi." He rubbed the back of his neck, still gazing at me.

"You look nice," I said, resisting the urge to fan my warm face.

He glanced down at himself. "Better than a poke in the eye with a sharp stick."

Yeah, *way* better.

He nodded at me. "You look nice yourself."

I waved off his compliment. "If I had my way I'd be in jeans and a tee."

He seemed to like my answer from the smile he gave me. "I'd rather be in cleats and football pads. Shall we walk together?" He held out his arm for me to take.

My smile was instant. *What a gentleman.* "I'd love to."

"Have you always lived in Arizona?" he asked as we walked toward the elevator.

"No, my dad was in the military until I was a teenager."

"Oh, yeah. You said that already. You have brothers, right? No sisters?"

"I'm the only girl with three brothers. Two of them live in Arizona. Of the two, one lives with me and my parents. He's the youngest and is savin' money by livin' at home. My brother, who is just younger than me, is in the military. I haven't seen him in over a year, so I miss him to the moon and back. My oldest brother is the only one hitched. He has the cutest baby boy who's now almost one. How 'bout you?"

"Two sisters, one brother. All younger and in school."

"Do they live close by? To you—in Arizona, not here in the sea, of course." That was stupid. Of course they wouldn't live in Europe.

He chuckled, adding to my humiliation. "They still live in Texas."

"So, do you dance?" I asked and we stepped out of the elevator.

His brows raised and his face flushed red.

"I just ask because I heard that some football players take dance classes so they are light on their feet, or somethin' like that."

"Yeah. I did take dance classes. My coach in high school insisted we take ballet and ballroom."

My phone chimed but I ignored it. "No kiddin'. My mama taught ballroom dance classes for years. Now she spends her time being a grandma."

He grinned and opened the outer glass door to the club. "My aunt once said that being a grandma is a reward for not killin' your kids when they were younger."

I laughed. "I suppose so."

Our conversation ended there, mostly because the loud beat of the music made it hard to hear each other without shouting. Plus, as soon as we walked in, Josie grabbed Preston's arm and pulled him into the crowd to dance.

Ivory stepped up to me and rolled her eyes, leaning in to be heard. "A leech, that one."

I nodded and walked with her to the booth where Delany and Trisha chatted. Koa joined us and asked Ivory to dance. I watched them on the dance floor, appreciating that Koa seemed to know how to dance and I wondered if all the Nighthawk boys knew how to cut a rug. Delany and Trisha left me alone to sit through a few songs. A man I hadn't seen before approached and asked me to dance. He had a nice smile, and I guessed he would be about ten years older than myself. I agreed and let him lead me to the dance floor.

By the time I was finished dancing with him I'd nicknamed him Handsy McGonnagetslapped. Three times I had to lift his hands higher and off my butt. When he asked to dance to the next song, I declined and returned to the booth. He stuck to my side, trying to chat with me. When I was about to make an excuse to leave, Preston saved me by asking to dance.

"Thanks for rescuin' me." I had to lean in and holler next to his ear.

His breath next to my ear jolted my heart. "Anytime. Not a fan of him, huh?"

"Not at all." The song we danced to was upbeat and fun. I couldn't stop laughing at the moves Preston and his buddies were busting out.

The song ended and the DJ spoke into the mic, his Latin accent strong and adorable. "Who here knows how to salsa dance?" I raised my hand along with Preston, Delany, Ivory, Koa, Mallory, and a few other people. Preston smiled at me and winked. My insides fluttered with delight.

"Okay. We are doing a competition, si? All the dancers who know how to dance find a partner. The best couple wins free drinks."

Koa slapped his hands then asked Ivory to dance. "We've got this made."

"Oh, yeah?" Preston took my hand and pulled me close to him. "Think again."

I laughed. "I suppose that's you asking me to dance again?"

He nodded and the music started. Preston spun me out so we stood a few feet away. I swayed my hips and used my index finger to gesture to him to come to me. His brows rose and a smile grew. We met in the middle and fell into step together. People shouted and cheered us on. Not only did the heat rise in my body from moving, but also appreciating the way Preston's hips moved.

The song ended with Preston pulling me into a hug and laughing. "You're fantastic!"

"You ain't so bad yourself, honey. You're the best dance partner I've had in a long time."

"The winner," the DJ cut in over the mic, "is this couple right here." He pointed at Preston and me.

I jumped up and down then gave Preston a high five. "Yeah!"

Another song started, but I needed a break. "I need to sit this one out." I fanned my face.

Preston led me to the booth. "You want that free drink?"

"Chardonnay, please."

He left and a few others in our group joined me. When Preston returned his buddies gave him crap for winning. Noah shook his head. "You only won because Billie here can dance."

"Not just dance, but she can *daaance*," Koa said, then pointed at me. "You and me, next dance."

"I'll be there with bells on," I answered and noticed Josie was shooting daggers at me from across the table with her heavily lashed eyes.

"Do you cha cha?" Koa asked.

Ivory waved at me. "Her mama was a dance instructor. She can do it all."

"I wanna dance with you too." Noah winked. "Any girl who can dance like you can is an animal in b—" Koa slugged Noah in the arm, but my attention was taken away from the *boys* to where my phone vibrated against my leg. I pulled it out and saw I'd missed two video calls from Mama and received about two dozen texts by about a dozen different people. "What the…"

"Is something wrong?" Preston asked in my ear.

"I don't know." I checked the first message and felt Ivory's eyes on me.

Holy cow! Congratulations, honey! That was from my assistant, Candace.

You did it sweetie! Way to go! That and many more similar texts were from Mama.

You did it! I can't believe you're a billionaire now!

That was from my project manager who sent the text with a link to the sales report. My jaw dropped and my hands shook. I held the report out to Ivory to see. I pointed to the text that stated that I was a billionaire, in case she didn't understand the full measure of my disbelief and shock.

"What! You're kidding!" she screamed.

I laughed and slid my phone back into my clutch. "Y'all, it's time to celebrate! Legion Games just broke the record for most games sold. Drinks are on me!"

"Does that mean you get a raise?" Delany called over the noise.

"Something like that." I shouted back.

The men cheered and hollered. The three other women looked confused but smiled happily. Drinks were ordered and passed around, but I couldn't help but notice a slight frown on Preston's face.

Wait. Didn't he like Legion Games?

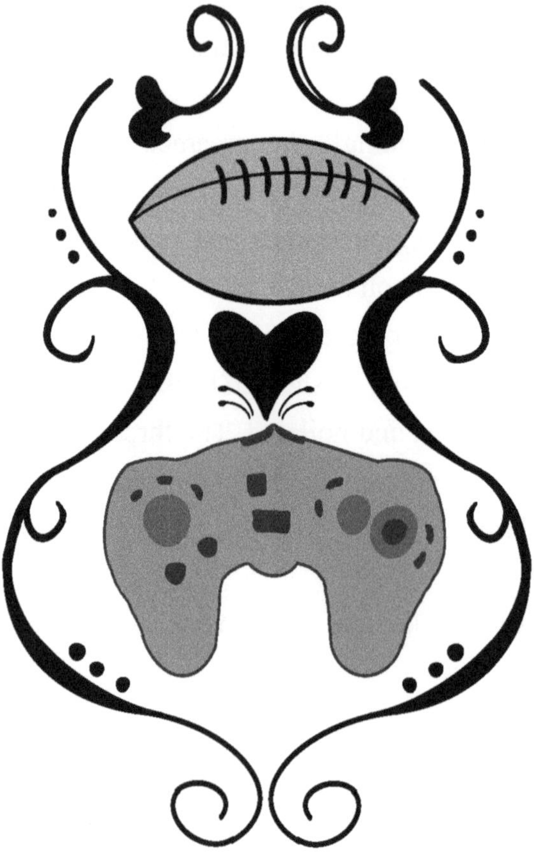

Four

Preston

Q: What's it like working on a cruise ship?
A: It has its ups and downs.

When Billie called out that she would buy the second round of drinks, that's when I leaned over and tapped Delany on the shoulder. We both exited the booth and walked to the other side of the room by the bar. "What's up?" he asked, scratching his curly head.

"I don't think we should allow Billie to keep buying our drinks."

"Why not? She's obviously thrilled about her company's success. What does she do for them anyway?"

"I don't know. Something techy. She lives with her parents, so she can't make enough to afford to buy everyone's drinks all night." I leaned my back against the bar and rested my elbows behind me. A woman walked by and gave me a flirtatious smile. I nodded without smiling.

"Then we should offer."

"I'm gonna." I walked to the bartender and gave him my card. We both made arrangements to pay for the drinks that were ordered for our table. When I headed back to the table Josie met me halfway and grabbed my arm.

"Dance with me." She didn't give me a chance to say no and led me into the crowd. Josie grabbed at the sides of my shirt, pulling herself into me and swayed her hips. Heat crept up my neck to my ears at the intimate way she wanted to dance. If my mama was watching, she'd have given me a nice goose egg on my head for dancing so close. I didn't quite know what to do with my hands until I decided enough was enough and gently urged her into a spin to get her away.

When the song ended, I leaned into Josie's ear. "I've got to find Billie. I owe her and Ivory a dance."

She pouted her bottom lip out. "What about me?"

"Later." I tried to smile to ease her mind. "Noah will dance with ya." I grabbed onto Noah's arm as he walked by and yanked him between us.

Josie latched onto his arm and leaned in.

Phew! I found Ivory first and asked her to dance. When I commented on her skills, she told me she'd learned from Billie's mom. "Did you and Billie grow up together then?"

"She and my older sister were best friends since middle school, but I tagged along with them for years," she called back over the music.

I caught onto the *were* part. "And now they aren't?"

She shook her head no, but didn't elaborate.

"She seemed really excited about her work's success," I said.

Her smile brightened like there was more to the news. "Yes. It's really exciting."

Billie came rushing up to our side, holding up a phone that looked like someone was calling. She yelled something about talking to someone. Ivory nodded then turned to me. "Sorry. I've got to take a call with Billie. We'll be back soon."

Mallory jumped in at that moment and asked to dance, so I tried to keep my attention on her and not on the redhead leaving the room.

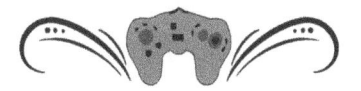

Billie

I tapped on the photo of Cassy and waited for my mama to pick up. This call and all the others were going to cost a ton, but it was worth paying for satellite phone access. Not that it mattered much that I had the money to pay for it. The screen on my phone changed and my mama's face came into view. "Hi, Mama!"

"I can't believe it! You're a billionaire now! It's all over the media and neighbors are callin' and everythin'."

"Hi, Sugar." Dad's face came into view, and he waved.

"Hi, Dad. Is Cas there?"

"She's sittin' on Malcolm's lap." Mom angled the phone to the sweet little girl on her uncle's hip. I waved at her and my brother. "Hi, baby!"

"Look, it's Mama!" my mom said and held the phone closer.

"Mum. Mum," Cas mumbled.

"She started saying 'mom' while you've been gone," my mama said.

"What!" I screeched. "And I missed it?"

"Let me see my niece." Ivory held her hand out for the phone. Instead of giving it to her I put my arm over Ivory's shoulders and held her closer so we both could be seen. "Hello, baby!" Ivory waved. "It's your favorite aunty!"

Cas's chocolate-colored cheeks looked so chubby I wished I could kiss the life out of them. My heart ached at being away from my adopted daughter. "Oh, honey! I miss you! Mama misses you, honey!"

"She just finished eating breakfast, so she's got food all over her cheeks," Mama said as she struggled to keep hold of the phone. Cas's face inched closer to the point her tongue nearly licked the camera. "Yuck, honey. Don't eat the phone. Holy cow! How is her grip so strong?" Mama fought the phone away from my baby's death grip then held it up so we could see her again in Malcolm's arms. Since she couldn't have the phone, she fisted a handful of Malcolm's hair. He yelped and tried to free himself.

"Hi, Malcolm." Ivory waved.

"Hi, Ivory. Your ex is stupid and you're better off without him," Malcolm responded, and Ivory's smile faltered.

"Thanks for that," I said wryly to him. "You better not be feeding my baby licorice again."

"I'm not! Jeez! Let it go, will ya?" He shook his head then let Cas down to the floor, holding her by the hands so she didn't topple over.

"She'll be walkin' soon," Mama said. "I still can't believe you're a billionaire."

"Is there anything in the news about my baby?" I asked, worry freezing my heart.

"No. You've done a fantastic job keeping yourself out of the limelight, so there's nothing personal out there yet."

I sighed with relief. "Good. When I get home, we'll celebrate by picking a bunch of charities to donate to."

"Dad said he's excited to help you with that," Mama said, pointing the phone his way. He gave a thumbs up then continued reading his book.

"I've gotta go now, Mama." Blew a kiss to my baby who looked at me in the camera and mumbled, "Mum." My heart burst and my arms ached to hold her. "Give my baby lots of kisses."

"I will, sweetheart. Have fun and be safe."

"I will." I reluctantly hung up. "Oh, I miss her."

"I do too." Ivory put her arm on my shoulder. "What was that about licorice?"

My eyes widened from the horrible memory. "Malcolm got this brilliant idea that he needed to share a package of red vines with Cas. She threw it all up all over the back seat of the van. Then later she had red poop blowout up her back. Worst experience ever."

"Hopefully Malcolm helped you clean it up."

"I wish. He was already long gone when that happened."

"She's looking more and more like my sister every day," Ivory said, her smile disappearing.

"Yes, she is." I slid my phone back into my clutch and opened the outer door. "Let's dance a few more then call it a night."

"Deal." She pointed at me. "But one of your dances has to be with Preston and the other with Noah."

"Why?"

"Because Preston keeps asking about you. And I think Noah wanted a dance." She wiggled her brows and smirked. "I think Preston likes you."

Wait. What? He's interested? I brushed away the idea and the butterflies the thought brought. "Whatever. It's only because I can dance." We opened the inner door and headed in to find some dance partners before they grew too drunk.

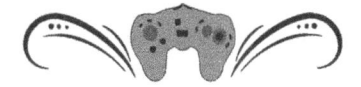

Billie

The handheld fan I waved in my face did very little to stifle the heavy humidity and the one hundred degrees plus temperature. And it was only nine in the morning. "I think I'm going to die, then melt into a puddle, then fizzle into a gas, then die again."

Ivory looked at me funny. "What? I think the heat is affecting your brain, honey."

"It's affecting everything." We moved another few steps toward the bus. The line moved steadily but not fast enough in this kind of heat. "Maybe we should have skipped the excursion in Tunis. I mean, is it worth turning into a gaseous state to see some Roman ruins?"

"It wouldn't be so bad if we didn't have to fully cover our bodies." Ivory wiped the sweat off her forehead and stepped forward again. We'd been warned before exiting the ship that the safest option for women visiting the city would be to cover up as much as possible.

Hands clamped down at my waist, causing me to scream and jump a foot in the air. "Good golly mud pies!"

Noah chuckled in my ear and placed an arm over my shoulders. "Hi, darlin'. Lucky us. We're all on the same excursion." Koa, Delany, and Preston all stepped up beside us. The people behind us grumbled something about them cutting in line.

"Hey, guys," Ivory said as I said, "Hello."

I lifted Noah's arm off of me. "Sorry. Too hot for touching, honey."

He chuckled and took my hand instead, turning so he faced me and slowly walked backwards. "Thanks for the dances last night. You know how to move, girl."

I tilted my head and shrugged one shoulder. "Thanks." My gaze went beyond him. "Watch it. You're gonna run—" His body slammed into the door frame— "into the bus."

Preston chuckled as he stepped onto the bus, and we all followed one by one. As soon as he sank into a seat, he locked eyes with me. For a second I thought I saw an interest or perhaps an invitation for me to join him in his eyes, but before I could react to it Noah grabbed my hand and pulled me to a seat next to him and across from Preston. Ivory sat beside Koa, and Delany ended up beside Preston.

"Tell me somethin' interestin' about yourself." Noah leaned in, pressing his shoulder against my arm.

I glanced around the bus, wondering why in the Sam Hill the AC wasn't on. "Well, I love video games and my family."

"What made you get into video games?"

"My brothers. If I hadn't started playing with them, I don't know if I ever would have been included in their lives. At least my oldest brother. He and I are the closest—at first, we weren't, but we are now. He taught me a bunch about computer programming and techy stuff. It's kinda all his fault."

"His fault you work for a gaming company?"

"Yep." I fanned myself more. "Now, I might not always be observant, but I see vents on the bus. They've gotta have AC, right?" The bus jerked forward. "Sorry." I tried to smile. "I get a little grumpy when I'm hot. And when I'm hungry. It's doubly worse when I'm hot and hungry. And triple worse when I'm in pain."

"You don't need to tell me you're hot. I knew that from the first day I met you."

Wow! He's a flirt and a half.

"Speakin' of first day we met…" He nodded in Ivory's direction. "What's with Ivory? She said this was supposed to be her honeymoon trip. What happened?"

My head jerked back. "She said that?"

"Yeah. How soon before the weddin' did they break up?"

"He walked away from her at the altar."

"Ouch. That sucks." He paused, studying me a moment while the bus drove into the city where traffic got heavier and heavier with no apparent method to the madness. There didn't seem to be any defined lanes or directions cars adhered to. "What about you?"

"What about me?"

"Have you almost been married? Had a serious boyfriend?"

I snorted, which should have given him the answer. "No. I've been focused on work and haven't had time." Plus, a vast majority of men were creeps. What would he say if I told him I'd never been kissed? Like *really* kissed. I glanced at Preston, who seemed to be listening in on the conversation by the way he leaned in and glanced our way.

"What about high school or college? No serious boyfriend?"

"I was the kind of girl who spent all my time with my nose in a book, learning important stuff and hiding from boys. I wasn't exactly sought after or even paid attention to." *Until the last few years when I'd started earning more than I could say grace over*. I didn't share that last bit with him. He absolutely didn't need to know.

"I find that hard to believe." Noah brushed his finger along my hand and forearm.

"I bet you were the guy in school that dated all the girls. You probably broke a lot of hearts. Am I right?"

He shrugged.

"Yes. He was," Preston answered. "Still is."

"No one asked you, Preston." Noah shot at him.

"Am I wrong?" Preston flung back.

"You didn't know me in high school," Noah countered.

Preston shrugged and I'd bet he had a good handle on the kind of guy his friend was. In short: Stay away from Noah.

Noah continued to ask questions, some I skirted around. It didn't take a degree in rocket science to figure out that to keep from having to share too much about me, all I had to do was ask about him. His favorite topic.

Ten minutes into the ride, a bang and jerk of the bus interrupted the conversation. The abrupt stop hadn't been enough to harm anyone inside the bus, since we were basically crawling through traffic.

"Did the driver just hit a car?" Noah asked.

Sure enough, it had.

"Do you think we'll have to go back now?" I asked. I'd figured the police would be called and that would take up all our time for the half-day trip.

Seconds later I had my answer when the tour guide stepped out of the bus door. He called out what sounded like a question to the other driver. Someone responded. The tour guide answered then the bus moved on ahead.

"Wow. Did that just happen?" Ivory said in wonder. "No police or anything?"

What surprised me even more was that our driver began performing a seven-point turn in the middle of eight lanes of packed traffic, heading back in the direction we had come from. The bus crawled a few more blocks at a snail's pace before we reached a clear spot in traffic.

At last we arrived at the destination. I stepped out and pulled out my phone to take all the photos I needed to remember the structure and architecture of an old Roman bath house, or recreation center. Ideas for another game started flipping through my head. Ivory stepped up to me and nudged me, just as I took a shot of a fallen column.

"I know that look. You've got ideas from this, haven't you?"

I grinned. "You know me well."

"I'm guessin' that as soon as we get back, you'll have your nose stuck in a sketchbook."

"No," I shook my head. "I can wait. I'm here to spend my time with you."

"*Riiight.*" She gave me a heavy eye roll.

"Cross my heart." I moved my finger across my chest.

"Would you like me to take a pic of you two?" Preston asked us.

"Sure." I held out my phone to him then put my arm around Ivory. He snapped a few, then looked at the screen of my phone. "That's a cute baby."

I snatched it away. "The cutest." I twisted away from him to look at the photo, so I didn't have to answer a possible question of who the baby belonged to. I wasn't ready to share her with everyone. It wasn't that I was ashamed, because that was far from the truth. It was more to do with protecting her. As my wealth grew my life became more public, and I didn't want to share her with the world. She was too special.

At the next stop we walked the shaded alleyways of shops in the city. Talk about rugs. Lots and lots of Persian rugs. I bought a few and set up shipment for them to be delivered to my home. We ended up getting separated from the guys, so Ivory and I—along with a few others on the bus—walked through the shops and enjoyed our girls-only shopping moment. I bought a few items for my parents and brothers, packing them in a bag I had to buy in order to carry it all back.

On the drive back I sat with Delany, who wanted to take a nap. Since I sat against the window the other guys couldn't chat with me unless they talked over Delany. I made a mental note to do something nice for him for giving me some reprieve.

When we arrived back at the ship, Delany spoke up for the first time. "So, anyone want to guess how hot it got today?"

"My guess is four hundred and sixty-two degrees," I answered. "Hot enough the hinges are meltin' off the doors of hell."

"That's specific." Preston chuckled behind me, and we made our way into the air-conditioned ship.

"Close." Delany laughed. "One hundred and seventeen with eighty percent humidity."

"No wonder. I drank two and a half liters of water and haven't needed to pee yet," Ivory said, shaking her head. "I think I sweat it all out."

"You and me both," I sighed, relishing the refreshing comfort of modern technology.

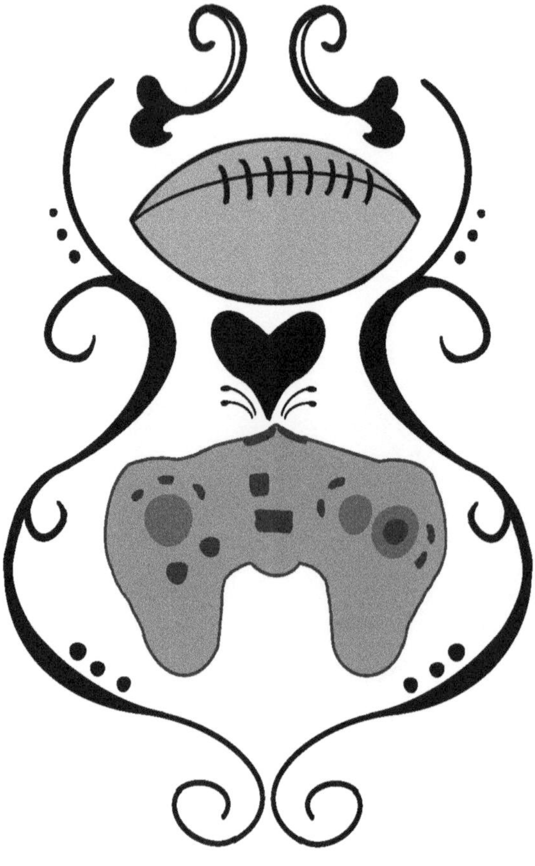

Five

Preston

I bought my wife a ticket to go on a cruise. It's no Titanic, but I'm optimistic.

Josie yanked on my arm, slid her hand down to mine, then pulled me to a grouping of cushioned chairs, ottomans, and end tables at the ocean view bar. "Careful!" I said, "You'll spill my drink."

"This is perfect. There are enough chairs for all of us." She sat and then patted the lounge chair beside her. I obediently lowered into the seat and placed my scotch and soda beside me on the table. We'd just finished dinner and ran into Ivory along the way to find somewhere to sit. After I'd asked about Billie, Ivory stated she had to make work calls, but Ivory promised to find her and met up with us.

When Koa sat in the seat next to me I glared at him, though he didn't notice. I had hoped to keep that seat open for Billie, but of course he couldn't read my mind. To keep Josie from trying to hold my hand I held my glass with both while we all laughed and chatted. Mallory and Trisha mostly chatted with Delany and Noah, so that left me and Koa to talk with Josie, who usually gave us a rundown of friends she knows and where they travel to. Also, fashion. A lot of fashion.

Not long later, Ivory arrived with Billie in tow. "I found her in the gaming room surrounded by boys. Surprise, surprise." Ivory dropped into the only available seat.

Billie dropped her arms to her sides in exasperation. "What?"

"I don't doubt she was surrounded by boys. But I might get jealous." Noah patted his lap like it was an option. She didn't take the hint and instead searched around for an empty chair to pull over.

There wasn't one and being that I had the only lounge chair I patted the spot in front of me. I shifted my legs away to make room. "You can sit here."

"Or you can sit on my lap." Noah smiled and winked at her.

I resisted rolling my eyes. Josie appeared like she was about to jump up and take the spot in front of me, but she was too late. Billie sat at the edge, leaning on one arm. "Thanks."

"Ivory and Billie need drinks too." Delany waved at a waiter nearby and asked him to come get drink orders.

Soon Billie had a drink with mint, and I couldn't help noticing how different she was from the other group of women. She wore jean shorts and a V neck tee that fit her nice form. Her casual clothing allowed her to relax and lay down on the lounge while we talked, her head resting a few inches from my leg. The other women all wore dresses that didn't allow for them to move without consequences.

The last of the daylight waned off on the horizon and soon the stars emerged. Billie's feet rested on the ground off the chair and her knees swayed side to side. The movement of them had me mesmerized and I had to consciously keep from admiring them.

"Look. You can see Virgo and Scorpius. Just barely though." Billie pointed in the sky.

"Oh, yeah." I said, tilting my head back to see.

"Back home we wouldn't see these constellations this time of night. Wouldn't it be cool to see the southern stars? I know I've never seen them."

"I bet it doesn't look any different than these," Josie said and pulled out her phone as if bored of the topic.

"Oh, they're different." Billie pointed out another set of stars and chatted about it to those who were listening. I found it fascinating that she liked a lot of the same things I did. I kept glancing down at her and when I could stand it no longer, I picked up a lock of hair and twirled it around my fingers. *Silk.*

Maybe the two drinks were getting to me and that's why I acted so bold to play with her hair, because soon I was running my fingers against her scalp to the ends of her hair. She didn't seem to mind, so I kept it up. A playful change came over me, so when she least expected it I stuck the end of her hair in her ear.

She giggled and plugged her ear, grinning at me. I stuck the hair in her nose. She squeaked and slapped my hand away. "You're just like my brothers."

I paused, debating inwardly. Do I want to be thought of as a brother to Billie? No. Absolutely not. But hearing her laugh was like a drug and I wanted more. I armed myself with two locks of hair, one in each hand and attacked. Billie swung her head this way and that, trying to prevent me from tickling her.

"You two are acting so juvenile," Josie huffed. My head snapped up in surprise. *Huh. I didn't know she knew that big of a word.*

Billie's phone rang, so I backed off with the tickling and instead twirled the hair in my fingers once again.

"Hi, Malcolm."

Malcolm? Who's Malcolm?

Her light tone turned clipped, and she sat up. "What? When?" she paused then continued, her voice edged with worry, "Is he okay?" Another pause. "What hospital?"

Ivory shot out of her seat and knelt beside us taking Billie's free hand. I put my hand on her shoulder to offer support to whatever happened. Her body shook as she listened.

"What about Cas? No, I want you there. Get a sitter." Her chin wiggled as if she were ready to sob. "Okay." Her voice cracked. "Call me when you know more. I don't care what time it is when you call. Just call." She hung up and let the phone drop into her lap where Ivory prevented it from falling to the deck floor.

"Billie. What happened?" Ivory asked. Everyone silently watched and waited.

"My dad had a heart attack." Billie broke down and sobbed. I slipped my arm all the way around her and pressed my head to hers. This totally sucks.

"Is Dad gonna be okay?" Ivory's voice equally shook. She said the word Dad like he was a father to her as well as Billie.

Billie nodded but couldn't seem to get the words out. She tried several times to speak and we all waited patiently. After a few minutes she managed to squeak out, "He's alive and going to the hospital. That's all I know."

"Is Mom with him?" Ivory asked.

Billie nodded, twisting her head into my chest to cry. I rubbed up and down her arm, wishing I could take the heartache away from her. Ivory struggled to keep it together, so I nodded to Koa, indicating that Ivory needed consoling as well.

Koa stood and pulled Ivory into a hug. Ivory held onto him and spoke into his chest. "He's like a dad to me too."

"I'm sorry. I bet he'll be okay since he's already on his way to the hospital," Koa whispered.

Billie wiped her face with the back of her hand. "Sorry. I'm just a big boob."

"That's okay. I like big boobs." The instant those words passed my lips I wished I could swallow them back in. My whole head heated, and I smacked my forehead with my palm.

Everyone busted up laughing, even the two weeping women. Never had my buddies laughed so hard. Noah even fell from his seat, holding his middle. I groaned and pressed the palms of my hands against my eyes. *Can I die now? Hurl myself over the edge of the ship into the sea?*

"I can't believe you just—ha! Ha! Ha!" Delany slapped his knee again, laughing harder.

Billie placed her hand on my knee when the laughter started to die down, which lasted about twenty minutes. My heartbeat quickened at her touch. "It's okay, Preston. I knew what you meant. And thanks for being sweet."

I gestured at Delany, Koa and Noah. "They're never gonna let me forget."

"Heck yeah!" Noah laughed and held up his glass. "To Preston, for always giving us reasons to laugh."

"And for liking big boobs!" Koa added.

Everyone lifted their glass to salute. Billie couldn't drink because she still giggled, holding the glass to her lips.

"Well, I'm officially mortified. I think I'll go bury myself now." I moved to stand up, but Billie held me back by squeezing my knee. My heart slammed against my ribs.

"No. Don't go." Billie shifted to face me more. *Wow! She wanted me to stay? Even after sticking my foot in my mouth?* "You can't go. Stay." She surprised me further by leaning against me. Her sweet perfume filled me, and I leaned into her.

"I can't believe I said that." I shook my head, still on fire from embarrassment.

"Well, it's true!" Noah stated and took a drink.

I fished an ice cube from my drink and chucked it at him. "You can shut up now, Noah."

He didn't shut up. Probably because he was getting drunk, and his mouth was running. "To all these fine ladies and their big boo—"

Delany slapped Noah on his gut, causing him to grunt. "You're wasted, man. How much have you had?"

Noah rubbed his stomach and cussed. "That hurt."

"It's better than a black eye from one of these women," I said, shaking my head.

Billie's phone rang and she stood, hurrying away to talk privately. My eyes followed her, wondering if she'd want someone to lean on.

"Well, I'm not going to be shy. It's good that men like big boobs. And *some* of us girls here are actually real in that department," Josie said with smugness that couldn't be missed.

Mallory narrowed her eyes at her friend. "Josie." Her voice held warning.

"Who are you suggesting has fake boobs?" Ivory asked with iciness lacing her voice.

Josie looked pointedly at Billie who had just returned and mostly likely had heard the remark, given her face went ashen. Josie raised her chin. "Some people are too vain, I guess."

Everyone looked at Billie, so there was no helping her embarrassment. Honestly, I didn't know why Josie thought she was fake. Billie looked perfectly proportionate. Why was I adding to her embarrassment by looking and thinking? *Idiot. Look away.*

Billie cleared her throat. "I'm gonna go talk to my family. See y'all later." She took a few steps then spun back to face Josie. "No. I need to say this…" she stood a little taller. "Some women have really good reasons for getting boob jobs and they aren't vain or selfish reasons. And they don't flaunt it like *some* women do."

Josie huffed and Billie walked away with her phone in hand.

"That was a cheap shot," Ivory said through her teeth toward Josie.

Trisha and Mallory shot up from their seats. Mallory took Josie's arm and pulled. "Come on, Josie. You've had a few too many."

Josie swatted her hand away. "Leave me alone. I'm fine. I know! How about we go dancing." She grabbed my arm. "Preston, will you dance with me?"

"I don't think so." I shook my head. She pouted.

"I'll dance with ya." Noah stood and sauntered off with the three women. I relaxed, glad to be rid of them.

"Sorry about that," I said to Ivory, rubbing my neck.

"How is it your fault?" she asked.

"I started it all by putting my foot in my mouth." Heat rushed in my ears again, just thinking of it.

"Again, not your fault. Billie is right. Some women don't have the privilege to have what they want and where. I probably shouldn't be tellin' ya this, but she was born without tissue that grows. The doctors don't know why and for all of her youth she was teased. So, it's a bit of a touchy subject for her. And I don't think it's wrong for her to want to feel and look sexy." Before anyone could respond she stood. "I'm gonna go check on her. Maybe we'll see you around later."

The three of us that were left fell quiet. Koa slapped Delany's leg. "What should we do?"

He shrugged.

All I could think of was helping Billie and wondering if her dad was okay. I stood. "I'm gonna go make a pit stop. I'll see y'all later."

Billie

I swung my cabin door open, surprised to see Preston on the other side standing in the hall. "Oh, hi." *Holy cow! Why is he here?*

"Who is it?" Ivory called from behind me.

"Preston," I answered and stepped aside to let him in.

"I was just coming to see how your dad is doing," he said and entered, taking up all the space.

Oh, good golly! How sweet is he? I could just kiss him. "I don't know yet," I answered and rubbed my arms, consoling myself. *Wait. Did I just say I'd kiss him?*

"It's kind of you to come check on her, Preston." Ivory smiled and patted the bed. He joined her, looking a bit awkward by rubbing his hands over his legs.

"She's been pacing since I got here." Ivory waved at me. I shot her a look of annoyance.

"Maybe she needs some distraction." Preston's eyes followed me.

I paused. "Maybe you're right."

"We could go dancing." Preston stood and nodded at the door.

"I'd like that," I answered. "But I don't want to get all dressed up."

"There's nothing wrong with your shorts and tee." Preston's cheeks colored a bit. His gaze darted around the room as if he tried not to stare at me.

"But Josie and her friends will be there," Ivory said, looking a bit dejected.

Preston's face fell. "Oh, yeah. That woman has claws." He shivered as though she had her talons around his neck.

Ivory laughed. "Maybe if you two," she pointed at me and Preston, "act more like you like each other she'll have no choice but to back off."

Preston sat taller and we both asked, "What?"

Change the subject. Change the subject! "I would rather not be somewhere so loud that I can't hear my phone." I lowered myself on the bed next to Preston.

"Maybe we just need to go for a walk," Preston suggested. "Or there's the comedy show."

"I'm game for either," Ivory said. "Do you think Koa and Delany will want to join us? I know that Noah is already occupied, or I'd invite him."

"I bet they would. Let's see what they think too." Preston stood and extended his hand to help me up. My heart raced again when our fingers briefly intertwined. We stepped out of my room, and Ivory offered to text Koa—apparently, she already had his number.

"I'm gonna go meet Koa. They're getting dessert at the buffet. I'll meet you back on the deck where we were earlier."

"Sounds good." I waved at her then Preston and I headed back to the grouping of chairs under the stars. We settled into our seats and began chatting about constellations, the teachers we liked or disliked in school, and then the conversation shifted to football.

"I like football," I said. "I've been to a fair number of high school games because my brother played. But I honestly couldn't tell you much about the rules or position of the players."

"Do you think you'd like it if you learned about it more?"

"Yeah. I think so. I don't know if I'd like watching on TV as much, but watching a live game is fun."

He patted my hand then pulled it away too soon. "You should come to one of our games. I'll get you some tickets."

"You don't have to do that. I can pay for them," I said, turning toward him in my chair, sitting with my knee bent to my chest.

"It doesn't cost me anything, so don't worry about it."

I had no idea if that was true or not, so I decided to simply say,

"Thanks. I'd like that." I twirled my hair in my fingers, thinking about when he did the same and wondering if he'd do that again. "When does the season start?"

"Spring training has already started—and let me tell you, keeping up with our exercise routine is difficult on a cruise. We're supposed to be back to practice the day after we get back. Hopefully we're not too jet lagged. Coach would hang us if we didn't show."

Our conversation shifted again to music, and Preston got the brilliant idea to start listening to a random playlist of ballads from the 60s to the 90s. We made a game out of it where neither of us looked at the title or band and tried to be the first to guess the song or band. We also got points if we could sing any portion of the song before the other one knew. We both laughed until we cried when I shared what I thought the lyrics to *Africa* by Toto were. Apparently, the words were not "I catch the waves down in Africa."

We talked for an hour before either of us wondered where Ivory ended up. I shot her a text and found out she was hanging out with Koa in the hot tub. I sent her an emoji with the heart eyes in response. "Do you wanna go meet up with them?" I asked.

Preston shrugged. "Nah. I'm good talking with you."

My face warmed. *He liked talking to me!* I scrolled through my notifications on my phone, wishing someone from home would contact me. "It's really getting late, but I don't think I can sleep until I've heard back from my family."

"I'll stay up with you," he said.

I smiled at him, loving that he didn't mind being with me. "You will?"

"Yeah."

My phone rang and I answered it before the first note finished. *What perfect timing.* "Yeah?"

"Dad's gonna be okay." Mom's words had the immediate

calming effect I needed. Every muscle in my body relaxed.

"Oh, thank goodness." All the stress and worry dropped from me, releasing me from its piercing grip.

"They're keeping him for a day, maybe two to do some testing, but he's gonna live." She sounded worried but there was great relief in her voice. She went on to share all that the doctor said then insisted that I not worry and forced me to promise I wouldn't come home early. When I hung up I was so wired and started to pace again.

Preston stood and took my hand. "Come on. You need to get some of that energy out."

"Where are we going?" I asked.

"Dancing. I'm willing to bet Josie has drunk enough she's passed out in her room, so we won't need to worry about seeing her at the club."

"You're probably right." My heart had already started a dance in my chest from him holding my hand and not letting go as we walked the length of the ship to the club room. We entered and got a drink at the bar first to help calm me.

We didn't see any of our group, so we danced all of the songs we wanted together. And had a blast. We got another drink and tried shouting a conversation but couldn't hear well enough to understand. At one point an upbeat Latin song played, and our hips swayed together. I leaned my back against his chest and his hands rested at my hips. His breath was at my neck, and it started doing funny things to my body. My heart felt alive and very aware of his body moving against mine. His lips touched my neck under my ear, causing my heart rate to increase.

Oh, dear. What am I doing? I hardly know him.

Even with the warning thoughts, I spun around, gazing into his eyes. His hands slid around my back and down to my swaying hips. His eyes dropped to my lips then mine followed suit and lowered to his. Our bodies slowed but my blood pumped harder. He was a breath away.

Abort! Abort! You've had too much to drink and you're emotional. Get out! Back up the tonka truck! Abort!

I stepped away. "I think I'm getting tired now."

His dazed eyes came back to life, and he nodded his agreement. "It's late. I'll walk ya back."

We left the club and walked back silently, but holding hands. Given that his room was next to mine, he of course would be walking me back all the way, but as we got closer to my door my nerves went into overdrive. Would he want to kiss me goodnight? Hopefully, he didn't expect to be invited in. Though with the way our bodies moved together he might be thinking that's where things were heading. *Oh dear*.

What do I do? My lack of kissing experience had my stomach in knots with worry.

"I had a good time tonight." Preston leaned against the wall next to my door.

"Me too." I smiled at him and opened my door, but kept it mostly shut. "Thanks for helping to keep my mind occupied."

"I'm glad I could help." He reached up and tucked a lock of hair behind my ear then trailed his fingers down my neck. My eyes rolled for just a second and I took a deep breath. He lifted my hand to his lips and kissed it. "I'll see you tomorrow."

"Yeah." *Do I have knees anymore? They're still there, right?*

He stepped away and smiled. "Goodnight."

"Goodnight, Preston." Once the door shut, I leaned heavily against it and held my hand to my heart. *Oh, help me. I think I like him.*

Six

Preston

What did the gamer say when they were told they had to spend the next year inside their home, physically isolated from the rest of the world? What's the catch?

I stood frozen, holding my breath as if that might help me hear whether Billie was awake and moving on the other side of the wall. I'd been up for over an hour, already spent time in the gym, and now, freshly showered and dressed, I found myself wondering if I'd run into Billie at breakfast. *How can I miss her already?* Regardless, I couldn't hang around here any longer. I left the room and headed down the elevator to the dining hall.

"Preston!"

I jumped as if claws hooked themselves into my back at the sound of Josie's voice. I turned, wishing I'd not been seen. "Hi." Perhaps if I kept my responses short, she'd become disinterested.

Mallory and Trisha waved, giving me flirtatious smiles to match Josie's. "Where're the guys?" Trisha asked.

"They were still working out in the gym when I left. I started a bit earlier than they did. Have you ladies had breakfast?" *Oh, please say you have.*

"We have,"—*phew!*—"but we can come sit with you while you eat so you're not alone." *Shoot!* Josie grabbed my arm and walked with me to the table where I hoped to find Billie and Ivory. To my joy they were both there, eating and looking at something on their phone.

"Look at this one." Billie held the phone toward Ivory. Neither of them noticed us yet, so they continued their conversation. "This house is three million but has twelve bedrooms and ten bathrooms."

"You should go look at that one," Ivory stated.

What was someone like Billie looking at million-dollar real estate for?

Before I could voice a question Josie lowered herself into the booth and pulled me in after her so she sat between me and Billie. "What are you looking at, honey?" she asked Billie.

Billie's wide eyes, flushed cheeks and the rush to put away her phone had me wondering if she was hiding something. "Nothin'. Just lookin'."

Ivory shot her a look then smiled like nothing happened. "We just like to look at house listings for fun."

"Find anything interesting?" I asked, looking through the breakfast menu, but keeping my eye on her. *Did she enjoy her time last night? Was she glad to see me again this morning?*

"It's all interestin'," Billie stated with a smile. "That's why I look."

The smile directed at me was encouraging, right?

"What are you gonna do today?" Josie asked Billie and Ivory.

"Billie and I are gonna visit the spa and get a much-needed massage," Ivory answered.

"Really?" Mallory tilted her head in confusion. "I heard massages were sold out before we even boarded in Spain."

"They were. We booked it in advance," Billie answered and

took a bite of her eggs Benedict. "This is so good. Y'all have to try this."

I resisted licking my lips, thinking not of her food, but her lips. "It looks good. I think I'll order it." As if on cue our waiter, Gerold, arrived and took my order. As I asked about the exotic fresh fruit, I couldn't help overhearing the conversation with Josie and Billie.

"I'm a little surprised you're getting a massage. I assumed you didn't make enough to afford such a thing." Josie waved at Billie's faded tee shirt and shorts as if evidence that she didn't have money. Her comment irked me, and I wasn't sure why.

"Well, sometimes you just have to treat yourself and splurge a little," Billie answered with narrowed eyes.

Billie's phone buzzed so her attention was drawn away from Josie. Josie whispered to Mallory and Trisha, but loud enough for me to hear. "You know, those who can't afford luxuries should leave such things to those who can. It's better they don't know what they're missing."

"Yeah," Trisha responded with an air of importance.

Billie tensed, and the eye roll that followed made it clear she'd overheard. She took her last two bites in a hurry then asked Ivory, "Are you finished? I'd like to respond to a few emails before our appointments."

Ivory ignored Billie and addressed Josie, "Ya know, if ya wanted a massage then maybe you should have acted like an intelligent person and booked one in advance. But I suppose that's a long stretch for you." She ducked under the table in order to get out without waiting for us to move. Josie gasped and huffed with shock and resentment. I quickly jumped up to let Billie out, who followed.

When the waiter walked by, I flagged him down and asked for my meal to go. Now that the only two decent people were gone, I had no reason to stay. Unfortunately, Josie and her goons didn't have a reason to stay either, so I had to quickly come up with an excuse to be alone. My mind went to the real estate that Billie had looked at earlier. "I need to email my realtor."

Josie held my arm, slowing my escape. "Are you buying a new home?"

"It's all up in the air right now. Maybe." I freed myself from her grasp and stood. "I better go."

Run! Don't look back! Or she'll send her flying monkeys after you!

I walked fast, hoping they wouldn't think I was rude, only urgent. Some women, when upset, could get ugly and mean. Josie seemed just like one that would, and I didn't want to be stuck on a ship with no escape. Better to keep her at arm's length, unaware of my disinterest than blatantly tell her I couldn't stand her.

I made it to safety along the deck where lounge chairs were scattered about. A color of bright red caught my eye, and my smile grew at the sight of Billie and Ivory resting on a couple of seats. Billie held a laptop on her legs, moving to a beat I could faintly hear from where I stood. I headed their way, debating on whether I should intrude or keep walking by.

Ivory's wave for me to join them made the decision easy. She gestured to a seat. "Hey, honey. Come join us."

Billie's eyes brightened when I caught her attention. "Hi. I see you escaped."

I laughed. "Barely," I held up my to-go container, "and with food."

Billie waved for me to sit beside her. "Have a seat. You can chat with Ivory and keep her company while I do boring things."

"She's supposed to be on vacation, but she keeps getting drawn to her computer like a gnat to a light." Ivory shot a dirty look at Billie.

"If you recall, I wasn't supposed to be on this trip. I shouldn't be taking this time off as it is."

Ivory's voice softened. "I know. I'm sorry."

Billie sat forward and took Ivory's hand. "No. I'm sorry. I shouldn't have brought that up."

Ivory waved. "It's fine. I can't hide from it." She looked at me and tucked her feet under her. "What excursion are you and the guys doing tomorrow when we get to Roma?"

"Well, we argued over what we were gonna do until it was too late, and now they're booked. So, we're considering going out on our own and seeing what we can see," I answered and took a bite of my eggs. "You're right, Billie. This is really good."

She looked up from her laptop and grinned. "Told ya so."

"Oh, her three favorite words," Ivory said, then laughed when she dodged Billie's attempt to slap her leg.

"Are not." Billie's smile and tone told me she loved the banter.

"You really shouldn't go out on your own," Ivory said once Billie's attention returned to her work. "Traffic alone might prevent you from returning to the ship on time before leaving port, and they can't guarantee you a safe journey back."

I hurried to chew and swallow. "It's either that or sit around here."

"There's plenty to do here," Ivory said. "I heard they have a surfin' pool somewhere on board."

"Yeah, I was thinking of trying that today."

"Do you think it will be as hot as Hades like it was in Tunisia?" Billie asked without looking up from her laptop.

"It will be hot, but I doubt *that* hot," I answered and looked her over once again. The sun made her hair look ablaze with fire. "Is your hair a natural color?" I don't know what made me blurt out that question, but I felt like an idiot in doing so.

She smiled at me. "A girl doesn't get all these freckles without being a true redhead.

Ivory pointed at the blonde strip in the bangs. "The blonde is natural too. She was born with it like that."

Billie brushed a stray curl out of her eyes, using her hand to shield her face from the sun. "I better get out of the sun, or I'll be burnt to a crisp."

"I didn't get to ask earlier … How's your dad?" I asked.

Her easy smile faded. "Because of the time difference I haven't heard. I won't hear from them until tonight."

Without thinking I reached out and placed my hand on Billie's knee. "Let me know when you hear." How is her skin so soft? Just as I was about to pull my hand away she covered my hand with hers and squeezed my fingers.

"I will. Thanks for carin'."

Her smile did funny things to my heart again. How could someone affect me so strongly? I'd had a few girlfriends over the years, but none of them created such attraction in me.

A few minutes later Billie slapped her laptop shut and stood. "I better go get ready for our appointment."

Ivory held up her arm to check her watch. "But we've still got like thirty minutes, honey."

"I know. I need to take care of something, and I don't want to fry like a forgotten hush puppy in the pan. Do you want to meet there?"

Ivory shrugged. "Sure. I'll just chat with Preston a bit."

Billie patted my shoulder. "Careful, when she gets into a mood she can beat her own gums to death."

I laughed. "I can handle a talker. Thanks for the warning though."

I watched Billie walk away, enjoying the way her sway moved

her hips. When my eyes returned to Ivory, she smirked at me as if she knew something.

Uh, oh.

"You like her?" she asked and sat forward, picking up a bottle of water.

"Uh, sure. Anyone would." *That's the right answer, right?*

"Uh, huh." She pointed her water bottle at me. "But you *like* like her. Right?"

I sighed. "Maybe. But I'm not looking for any relationships right now." *Especially with gold diggers, which I still didn't know for sure that Billie wasn't.*

Her eyes narrowed. "Then leave her alone. She's very open and trusting. To a fault at times, and I don't want to see her get hurt."

"I have no reason to hurt her. I'll keep my distance."

She smiled and stood. "Good. I'll see you around."

Preston

I swung the door to my cabin open to see Noah standing in the hall, holding an envelope. "Looky, looky what I got."

I took a few steps to my dresser and held up a similar envelope. "Could it be that angels are smilin' down upon us?"

"Looks like." He stepped in and shut the door. He slid the note out and read. "You have been chosen for a personal tour of Roma. You choose the destination and how long to spend at each stop—can you believe it! And it says we're traveling by way of limo." He slipped the ticket back into his envelope and slapped it against his hand repeatedly. "Both Delany and Koa got one too."

"That's great! I was feeling sad enough to bring a tear to a glass eye that we wouldn't get a chance to see Rome." I slid my wallet in my pocket. "You ready for dinner?"

"Yep. Do you think we're gonna have a show too?"

"What? Are you talkin' about Josie?" I opened the door and led the way out into the hall.

"Yeah. She brings a little spice to things, don't she?"

I huffed. "I wouldn't call it spice."

"What? You don't like her? She sure likes you. But not for long if I can help it." He had that familiar gleam in his eye—the one that always seemed to land him in trouble with the ladies.

"She's no good for you, Noah." I shook my head and hit the down button on the elevator.

"Either her or Billie." He bit his lips and shook his head before continuing. "Man, that girl can dance."

When we arrived for dinner, Billie was sitting alone, looking at her phone. She jumped when I slid in next to her. Noah sat at her other side. "Y'all scared me."

"You're jumpier than I box full of crickets," I said with a chuckle. "Any word from your family?"

"Yeah. Dad's doing great. They're letting him go home tonight—which will be early morning for us." A smile tugged at her lips and I could see the relief in her eyes.

I used the excuse of this news to put my arm on her shoulders and ease her into a side hug. Would she pull away? Would she be good with my arm staying there? "I'm so glad. That means you're stickin' around?"

"Yeah. I want to be with him, but they insisted I stay behind."

Noah leaned in. "Well, I for one, am happy as a hog in mud you're stickin' around."

"Thanks. I think."

"Where's Ivory?" I asked.

"Restroom," Billie answered, then took a drink of her water.

"Speak of the devil and she appears."

Ivory approached, her eyes sparkling just as brightly as her smile. She wasn't exactly mischievous, but I could tell their relationship was close enough for some playful teasing.

"Are you sayin' I'm evil?" Ivory asked and slid into the seat beside me.

"If the boot fits." Billie laughed and winked at Ivory.

Familiar loud laughter brought our heads around to find Josie busting up at something Koa said. Delany, Mallory and Trisha walked with them and piled into the booth next to us. Well, everyone but Koa who stood wondering which table to sit at before deciding to join the others. I could tell he wanted a chance to sit next to Ivory. Maybe next time.

Noah slapped his envelope down on the table. "Looks like we'll be goin' on a trip tomorrow after all."

"Why?" Ivory asked.

"The four of us got a free personal tour of our choosing for Roma tomorrow," I explained.

"Hey! So do we!" Ivory said.

Josie angled herself to insert her head between mine and Ivory's. "Yeah, Delany told us. Mallory, Trisha and I are doing that too, so we should all plan to go to the same places."

Billie and Ivory shared a look.

"We totally should." Noah brightened, giving her a wi-five, something I call a high five from far away.

I wanted to reach across the table and throttle Noah. Why did he have to open his big mouth? Billie straightened in her seat, shooting Josie a look that mirrored my own frustration. "It might be hard to meet up if we're taking different cars."

"It's fine." I couldn't miss the ice in Josie's tone.

The waiter arrived to take our orders and flirt a little with Ivory and the girls at the other table. He might have flirted with Billie, but her attention was directed to her phone. Her brows were pulled together.

I leaned into her. "You okay?"

She lowered her phone before I could take a glance at it. "Yeah. Totally fine. Just looking at reports about work and stuff."

"You were pretty thrilled the other night about the success of the company. Do you like working for them?" I asked.

"I love it," she said with a big grin. "It's been my dream."

"It's good to love what you do. I guess we're both fortunate in that. But wouldn't you want to do something that offers a bit more money?"

"I'm not worried about that," she answered.

"Yeah, you're hot enough to marry into money. Ain't that right, honey?" Noah nudged her.

I rolled my eyes. Give me a break. I knew Noah, and he liked to reel the women in with promises of wealth and stability then run when things get too serious. I didn't know if she was interested in Noah, and he seemed to jump around between the women in the group like a gnat. Is Billie interested in him? Or me?

We all chatted through dinner then decided to hang out in the lounge for drinks before catching a show. The trapeze show was impressive but didn't give us a lot of time for talking, which Josie obviously wanted to do since she talked to me and Noah the entire time. I hadn't planned on sitting next to her, but I was practically hogtied.

When the show ended, we debated on what to do next. Half of us wanted to dance and the other half wanted to soak in the hot tub. When Ivory announced that the bar next to the adult pool had dancing, we decided on doing both. We set out separately to change in our rooms. Not for the first time I thanked the stars above that

Billie's room was next to mine so we could walk up to the pool deck together. When she exited her room, I had a hard time not looking her over, but I couldn't not notice the polka dot vintage two piece she wore with the wrap at her waist.

Not only was I incredibly attracted to Billie, but she was great to be around and sharp as a whip. She was definitely girlfriend material—maybe even something more. But the only thing that had me holding the breaks was whether or not she was a gold digger. At times I wondered, but other times she didn't seem to act like one. She didn't cling to me like Josie, or look at me like I was a piece of meat like Trish and Mallory did.

In my experience with women searching for their millionaire I found that they acted like they had money and wore high end designer clothing. Billie kinda was a mix of someone who acted and someone who didn't have money at all. I couldn't figure her out.

But I wanted to.

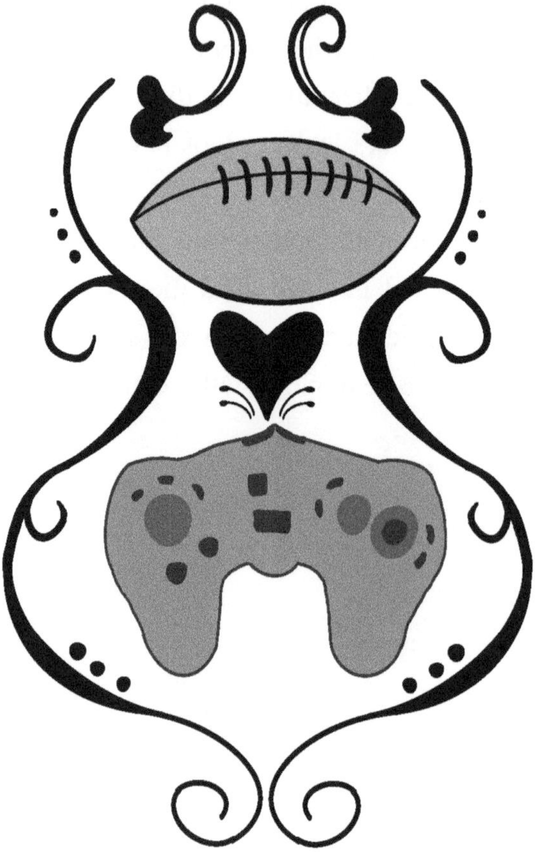

Seven

Billie

What did the football coach say to the vending machine? I want my quarterback!

The seat at the bar opened for two, so I stepped up with Ivory to order a Jägermeister with cream and ice. The bartender with the Italian accent winked at us then flirted as he created our cocktails. Before I could pay, Preston popped in between me and Ivory. "Drinks are on me."

"Oh, no you don't." I grabbed his forearm and tried to push him and his card away. "I found out what you did last time. I should be the one ordering you a drink."

He placed his hand at the small of my bare back, creating a clash of goosebumps and vibrations up my back, despite the heat radiating off of me from sitting in the hot tub. He moved his hand up to my hair where he tucked a loose lock up to the clip atop my head. "Well, how about you dance with me, and we'll call it even."

I rolled my eyes and Ivory laughed. "How is that fair?" Ivory asked.

He shrugged. "I think it's a win-win situation here."

"I'd dance with you regardless of whether you bought me a drink," I said, turning to him fully.

He placed a hand at the side of my knee and smiled seductively. "Really? What about two dances?" This boy was getting flirty, and I had to admit, I liked it.

I placed a hand to my ear at the song beginning over the speakers. "Hark. Do you hear that?"

His smile brightened. "Do you tango, perchance?"

Oh, melt my butter! That look in his eyes was hotter than a honeymoon hotel. I giggled and let him pull me onto the dance floor a bit further away from the pool. I hadn't put much thought into our attire. I'd already had a difficult time not wanting to stare at him, but moving my body against him with little clothing will probably be my undoing. I needed to keep my distance.

During the song he held me close for a few seconds, long enough that I could speak to him. "Where did you learn to dance like this?" I asked.

His brows moved up once as amusement lit his eyes. "My mom's Latin."

"Oh," I said breathlessly, and he leaned in, guiding me into a dip. When I raised my head again, I saw a flash of something in his eyes. Was it desire? Did he like me?

When the song ended, applause erupted around us. I was so into him and the way his hands pushed, pulled, and caressed me into each movement that I hadn't noticed we'd drawn a crowd. He held me close and kissed my cheek. "You are amazing."

My body reacted to his breath and words in my ear. Did it get hot out here? "I'm rubber, you're glue."

He laughed and guided me back to the bar where my drink waited.

"You two are the perfect dancin' couple," Ivory said and handed me my drink. She noticed me eying it. "Don't worry. I've kept my eye on it. It's safe."

Girl got my back.

Preston's brows pulled together. "Have you had someone mess with your drink before?"

"Yes. And the SOB didn't get away with it either," I said and shivered, thinking of the night someone thought they could kidnap me for ransom. The downfalls of being young, single, and rich.

Ivory grinned. "He was arrested without her even taking a sip. I saw him do it."

"Hence why I don't go to clubs anymore," I said. "Except for this cruise, of course."

"I'm sorry to hear that," Preston said. "I don't know why people become so desperate."

I shivered and took a few more long swallows of my drink.

"You want to return to the hot tub?" Preston asked, noticing my shiver.

"If we did, we wouldn't get word in edgewise," Ivory said, leaning toward the bar again. She waved at the bartender to get his attention. "Josie speaks ten words a second, with gusts to fifty," she said then shifted her attention to the bartender when he arrived. "I was wondering what your favorite drink is to prepare."

The bartender leaned in, giving her his smoldering look. "Does the lady like peaches?"

"Does a lost dog have fleas?" Ivory answered.

He laughed and rubbed her arm with the back of his fingers. "I have something very special for you." He winked and gathered the ingredients.

Ivory smirked and fanned herself.

"I bet he says that to all the girls," I said.

Preston nodded in agreement and placed a hand at my hip. He

brushed his thumb against my skin, sending a shiver of goosebumps across my body. I couldn't help but inhale sharply at his touch.

"I don't care if he does." Ivory batted her hand. "It's fun to flirt. I think this trip has really helped get my mind off—" She stopped, as if realizing what she was about to say. She sighed. "It's been good. Thanks, Billie."

I saluted. "Glad I could be of service."

Preston looked at me curiously. "Did you have something to do with her coming?"

Uh, oh. "Um. No. I—"

"A family member bought me my ticket for the cruise. Billie convinced me I still needed to go and took his place."

Ivory. I'm buying you a new Gucci Bag, I silently vowed.

"Some family member," Preston said and ordered a drink.

We returned to the hot tub and listened to Josie laugh and prattle on. Preston sat next to me with his arm resting behind my head. Each time he would try to start up a quiet conversation between us, Josie would interrupt with questions or comments directed to Preston that had no bearing to him at all. I moved in a bit closer, curious if Josie would still work her claws into him if it looked like we were together. My actions must have signaled my interest, because a moment later, he began drawing circles on my shoulder.

My body became hyper aware of every brush of his boardshorts, leg, or foot.

"So, I have a confession to make," Josie said, standing in the middle of the hot tub. The two other guys that we'd met tonight also sat with us and they both watched with interest. "I bought those tickets for you boys so you could go to Rome."

What the crap? How dare she! I shot Ivory a look I knew she'd understand. *Kill.*

Noah pulled Josie onto his lap. "Seriously?"

"Well, I couldn't let my best guys miss out on all the fun." Josie giggled and ran her fingers through Noah's hair.

"We pitched in too," Mallory added, looking between Trisha and Josie.

My blood boiled and my lips pressed into a hard line before I forced myself to look natural. The guys all congratulated the fakes on *their* gift.

I stood abruptly. "Well, I think I need another drink."

"I'll come with you." Ivory stood and followed me. I grabbed two towels and handed one to Ivory. Ivory pulled me to the end of the bar where there was enough space from a group of guys. "Why the look?"

"I'm so mad I could start a fight in an empty house," I hissed.

"Why?"

"I bought those tickets for the guys because I felt bad they couldn't go on the excursion. I even arranged so we had a large enough car to take us all. Now that the fakes have claimed ownership, we'll have to share the space and we won't get to go together."

"What a b—"

"Are these seats taken?" A guy close by pointed at the seat next to us.

"We're just getting a drink and heading back to the pool," Ivory said to him, her voice turning flirtatious. "But there's always room for more."

"You sound like you're from the southern states. What're your names?" he asked, sliding into the chair.

"I'm Ivory."

"Billie." I took my turn shaking his hand.

"Deacon," he said, then pointed at me. "You know, you look like that woman who owns Legions Gaming. The new billionaire that's all over the news."

I felt panic rise but tamped it down so it wouldn't show all over my face. *Crap*. He's seen all of the news reports that were going around. Each time I looked at my phone someone of my acquaintance sent me something new about myself. I was hoping it wouldn't catch up to me while on this trip. "No kiddin'. Too bad I'm not her. I could use a few extra dollars kickin' around my house."

Ivory whistled. "Billionaire, you say? Imagine havin' all that money." She slapped my shoulder. "You'd be able to get that kidney transplant you need."

I'd just taken a drink of my cocktail and nearly spewed it all over the bar top. Deacon looked me over as if I were sick and he'd catch it. "Oh. Sorry to hear you're not well." He stepped away. "Good luck with that."

"Thanks," I muttered, then smirked at Ivory when he toddled off. "Brilliant save." I lifted my glass to click with hers.

"He turned tail faster than a prairie fire with a tail wind," Ivory said, and we both giggled.

Preston

My fingers and toes were probably all pruned by now, but I didn't care. I was savoring the feeling of Billie sitting next to me, nestled comfortably under my arm. When she returned from getting a drink I continued to brush my fingers against her shoulder. If I was reading her right, she was liking it, so I slid my fingers up her neck.

I wasn't completely oblivious to Josie's attempt to try to weasel her way between us and that she had her sights set on me. But Noah kept her preoccupied most of the time. As time went on, I wanted to leave, but didn't want to go without escorting Billie. There were a few men trying to chat with her, seeming interested. One in particular gave me an uneasy feeling and didn't want her or Ivory to be left alone with him.

To my relief Billie spoke up around one in the morning. "Well, I'm one wheel down and the axle's draggin'. And since we've got to be off ship at eight, I'm headin' to bed."

"I'll go with you." I stood up with her. She shot me a look like she would tan my hide. I chuckled and held up my hands. "I didn't mean it that way. I'll just escort you back to your room. Ivory too, if she's goin' back."

"I'll escort her. She's not far from my room," Koa said and helped her to her feet.

We all said our goodbyes then dried off. I waited while Billie wrapped her skirt thingy—whatever those things were—around her waist and slipped on her shoes.

On our way back I wiggled my fingers through hers to take her hand. Her smile started my heart racing. All good signs. Things were going well and I could feel the current of energy between us. Did she feel it too? Had another couple not been on the elevator with us I might have even tested the waters by pulling her into a hug. Maybe brushed my lips on her cheek. Or a kiss on the neck.

But *no*. People.

We couldn't be alone. And I wasn't ready to be alone in a bedroom with her. I'd learned my lesson from rushing into a relationship with someone I couldn't trust.

When we stepped out alone in the hall she spoke first. "I'm glad y'all are gonna go on the excursion tomorrow."

"Me too. It was nice of Josie to buy those tickets for us. I didn't think of booking a personal tour."

For some reason Billie stiffened, and her smile no longer reached her eyes. "Yeah. Nice."

I chuckled, figuring she felt the same as me. "I know. She's not all that exciting to be around."

"She thinks the sun comes up just to hear her crow," she said, then flinched. "Sorry. I shouldn't have said that. My mama raised me to be kinder than that."

"It might not have been kind, but it's true."

We reached her door, and she turned to me. "Thanks again for the fun."

"You're the one that made it fun." I brushed her cheek like I'd wanted to all night. Soft. So very soft. I ran my fingers to the back of her neck then placed the other at her waist. She rested her hand at my chest, and I wondered for a moment if she could feel my erratic heartbeat. I moved in slowly, testing the waters, wondering if she would let me kiss her full, pink lips. Her chest moved like she was breathing heavier and her eyes dropped to my lips. A slight smile stole its way across my mouth.

"Hey, man." A hand slapped down on my shoulder. The stench of alcohol on the stranger's breath curled my nose hairs. "Yous two—woah!" He swayed until I caught him from falling. He huffed. "Yous twos don't know wheres they put my room, do ya?" His words slurred so much I almost couldn't understand him.

"No. Sorry," I said, then shot Billie an amused grin and I tried to keep him on his feet.

"They just up and hid my rooooom." He raised his hands and slapped them down again. "So rude."

"You look like you're vertically challenged," I said with a chuckle.

"What?" His eyelids slowly dropped. Oh, boy. This guy was gonna fall asleep right here if I didn't get him to his room. He scoffed, getting a few bits of spittle on my chest. *Gross.* "I'm not as drunk as you think I am." He laughed. "Didja hear that? I shhhwitched the worbs around. Ha! I'm hilrariousss."

"I think he meant to say I'm not as think as you drunk I am," Billie giggled.

"I better help him find his room," I said, regretting having taken my time earlier and not getting that kiss.

"You probably should." She nodded and opened her door.

I took her hand while holding the man up by the arm. I leaned in and gave her a quick kiss on the cheek. "I'll see you in the morning."

"Knock on the door and we'll walk down together."

I grinned. "That I can do. Goodnight, Billie."

"Her namesss Billie? Like Billie goat?" the man asked, then started making goat noises. I mouthed the word sorry to her before she shut the door, laughing.

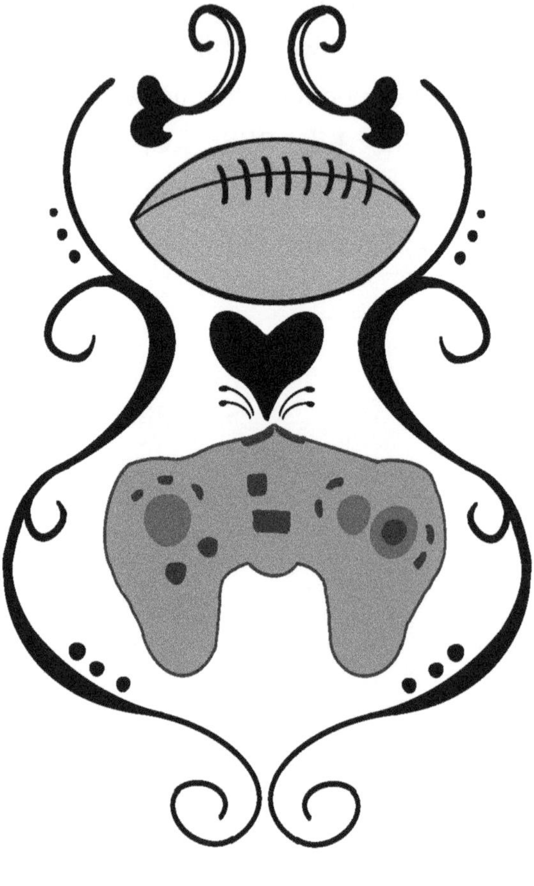

Eight

Preston

I'm not a player, I'm a gamer. Players get chicks.

A typical morning would have me spending a lot more time in the gym and taking a long shower afterward. But my time was cut short by the early departure time for the excursion and my anxiousness in seeing Billie again. I knocked on her door and bounced on my toes. I brushed a bit of fuzz from my white buttoned shirt I wore with my shorts.

Her smile greeted me, and I returned the gesture, taking a moment to admire her. I couldn't help but love the way her freckled legs peeked out from beneath her flowing summer dress. "You look nice," I said, trying not to sound too eager and stupid.

"So do you."

I stepped aside so she could join me. She slid a backpack on her shoulder. I pointed at it. "You might want to leave it here. There's a lot of pickpockets on the streets."

"It's completely empty. I'm only bringin' it to hold the water bottles for everyone."

"That's very kind of you, *Mom*," I said playfully.

She slapped my shoulder. "You won't be teasing when you're drier than a popcorn fart and dyin' of thirst."

I laughed and took her hand in mine. "So, where's your money if you're not carrying it in the bag?"

She grinned. "Top pocket." After giving her a confused look she pointed at her chest.

My face warmed. "Oh."

We arrived on time with everyone else and made our way down the long ramp off the ship. Once through the point check at the bottom, showing them our identification, we headed to the line of limos and other cars. Then came the awkward part of deciding where everyone would ride. I stuck to Billie's side like glue, not wanting to be separated from her. She took the initiative and pulled both Ivory and I into one car, then called over her shoulder for Koa to follow.

"But I wanted to be with Preston and Koa too," Josie whined and I got the feeling it was a common occurrence for her throughout her life.

I shot Noah a look asking for help. He nodded once and held his arms wide. "Hey, babe. All you need is me." He guided her away from the limo and wrapped his arm over her shoulders. Delany gave me a look like he wanted to choke me. This whole trip he'd gotten annoyed at Josie. If it weren't for her, I'd suspect he would have gotten along with Mallory, but I knew him well enough he wouldn't want to suffer through Josie's crap just to be with Mallory. But seeing the uneven numbers between the cars he chose to ride with Noah.

I owed him one.

To my delight Billie snuggled into my side on the way into the city. Having decided last night where we wanted to go, we watched eagerly out the window for any sign of Vatican City. Along the way we watched a few villas and vineyards go by. Billie pointed at one. "Look how gorgeous. I would love to live in a place like that."

"It's beautiful," I agreed.

"I want to buy a place like that one day soon." She turned to me. "Wouldn't you?"

Soon? For her? Not likely. "Maybe."

The car ride was longer than expected, but it was filled with good conversations. When we exited the car, our guide directed us toward the large buildings surrounding a square. My heart dropped when I saw the thousands of people in line to enter St. Peter's Basilica. Our other group found us. Noah had his arms around both Josie and Trisha, looking proud as a peacock. Josie kept shooting me and Billie dirty looks and glancing at our linked hands.

"Um. I think it's gonna take hours to get through this line," Billie said beside me.

"This way." Our tour guide and driver, Berto, waved at us. Without explanation we followed him past the thick, crowded line of people. I kept a tight hold of Billie's hand so if we got lost, we'd get lost together. Berto paused every few dozen feet to make sure none of us got left behind. The sun beat down on us as we made our way through the crowd until we reached the front of the line where security checked our bags and had us walk through metal detectors.

"Berto, I could kiss you right now for getting us through that crowd," Billie said with a sigh. "I'd be burnt to a crisp if I had to stay in that line."

Berto wiggled his eyebrows. "I won't refuse a kiss from a *bella dea*."

"A what?" she asked with her nose perfectly wrinkled up in confusion. I had a sudden urge to kiss her nose.

"*Bella dea*. Beautiful goddess." He winked and continued on.

She pulled me along with her and whispered, "Gross. He's like twenty years older than me."

I laughed and squeezed her hand.

Never in my life had I seen so many paintings or carvings. And to think they were all in one place. It took us a couple of hours to walk through it. And they saved the best for last. I heard Billie gasp when we entered the Sistine Chapel. By the time we reached the other side, admiring the grandeur of each painting on the ceiling and walls, I had a crick in my neck from looking up.

I was so far gone admiring the paintings I didn't notice until after we left the room that Billie had tears running down her cheeks. "What's wrong?" I asked, easing her closer and putting my arm over her shoulders.

"I've always wanted to see that for myself. It's way better than I imagined."

We all took as many photos as we were allowed through the tiny city filled to the brim with art and history. Next stop, we enjoyed an Italian feast in a hidden restaurant down a quaint, romantic alleyway. At least *romantic* was how Billie described it. Us four guys polished off the offerings. I doubt the restaurant owners knew how much a few professional football players could eat. We did have a little extra given that Josie complained and refused to eat the pasta, claiming that carbs were the devil.

When we returned to the cars, Josie loudly ordered everyone into different cars. She put up such a fuss we all agreed, though reluctantly. I ended up in a car with Mallory, Trisha, Noah, and Josie, who pressed herself at my side. I kept my hands grasped together between my legs, wishing for the Colosseum to arrive sooner than not.

Josie made me jump when she leaned in close to whisper in my ear. "You know, I just wanted to warn you about Billie."

"What about Billie?" I asked, wondering what she could

possibly know.

"She's a gold digger. I heard it from her own lips."

I narrowed my eyes. "What did she say?"

"She said that finding someone with money was more important than anything else." She wiggled her fingers through mine as my stomach dropped and my body tensed.

"Are you sure?"

"I'm not a liar. You can ask Trisha," she nodded toward her friend. "She heard too."

Trisha must have been eavesdropping because she nodded. "It's true."

"Be careful, because she's got her sights set on you." She squeezed my hand. "Haven't you noticed she's always looking at ways to spend your money? She's a woman who knows what she wants and how to get it. She might act like the girl next door, but she's got claws."

The same thing could be said about you.

I grew quiet and only joined in the conversation around me when necessary as I thought about her claim. She had a witness to what Billie said. And she was right about her looking at things outside of her means. Hadn't I found her looking at real estate in the millions of dollars? Hadn't she asked me on the way here about purchasing a villa in Italy?

Maybe Josie was right.

As much as I didn't want to admit it, I think she was telling the truth. And it hurt. But why? Had I already started having feelings for Billie? Did I care that much that I would get worked up over being deceived?

I should have held back. My first impression of her was the very thing she turned out to be. Why didn't I listen to myself the first day and stay away from her?

Billie

"Well, shoot. Would you look at that." I tilted my head back to stare at how giant the Colosseum stood among the busy streets of the city. I spotted the other group and stepped up next to Preston, slipping my hand in his. "People who live here drive by this everyday—like it's normal."

"Yeah." He pulled his hand away and folded his arms.

I thought it odd, since he'd been trying hard to always keep his hand in mine or an arm around me. I shrugged it off. Maybe he needed a break from being touchy. I handed him my phone. "Can you take a pic of me and Ivory?"

When I'd asked him before he'd happily offered. This time he gave me a soft, "Sure."

I stepped next to Ivory and posed for a pic with my arms out wide over my head. We did our best Vanna White for the next pose. I sensed something was off when Preston didn't comment or laugh at our silly poses. He ignored my questioning look.

We moved along, heading up the flights of stairs, pausing to take pics. Preston barely said a word to anyone, and he didn't seem to care when Josie hung on him. When I found him off to the side, admiring the view of the inside I nudged him with my shoulder. "Hey, anything wrong?"

"Nope. Just tired."

"Okay." *Not okay*. He didn't even look at me when he answered, then he walked away. *Definitely not good.*

I watched him join up with Noah and wondered what happened. *What had I done?*

"What's goin' on with you and Preston?" Ivory fell into step with me.

"I was just wondering the same thing. He's gone all cold on me."

"So, I haven't had a chance to talk to you yet since last night." Ivory paused and took a picture but continued to talk. "You were pretty lovey dovey with him in the hot tub and I'm wondering how far things went."

I sighed, thinking of how close we'd come to kissing. "I think he *was* gonna kiss me, but a drunk guy interrupted."

"Uh. Maybe the drunk spared you from more heartache than you would have had. That is, if Preston's changed his mind about likin' you, it's probably good."

"I guess."

"Trust me. It's better to have things end before it gets to the point where you're wearing the white dress and listening to hysterical parents fighting." The hitch in her voice tugged at my heartstrings.

I wrapped my arm around her, my heart breaking for her once more. It wasn't just her parents who had freaked out; her ex's parents had reacted just as badly. Honestly, I felt she had dodged a bullet by not being tied to that family. I sensed she understood that too. Even if it was difficult to be tossed aside.

Which was how I felt right now.

We didn't move beyond a small amount of cuddling. We hadn't kissed. We hadn't even claimed any relationship or emotional attachment.

So, why did it hurt? Why do I feel like I lost a close friend?

Things didn't get better. If I could have a nickel for each word he spoke to me I wouldn't even be able to buy a single taffy candy. We drove back with only Ivory and Koa in our car. I spent my time on the phone, trying to answer emails while Ivory and Koa got a little chatty.

I tried to ignore them.

We arrived back at the ship at six and still Preston didn't seem interested in conversing or even looking at me. When I arrived back at my room, I took a few moments for myself then went to Ivory's room. I knocked and was let in.

"Sorry about earlier. Hopefully, you didn't feel cut out of our conversation in the car," Ivory said.

"It's fine." I dropped onto the bed. "So, you and Koa?"

"Maybe. He's hot and nice, but I'm not ready to jump headfirst into somethin'. Even if he earns millions by running up and down a field."

"How very wise of you." I smiled, knowing this was a big step for her. She's always jumped from one relationship to another. That was until stupid Shay. *My friend is growing up!*

"Seriously though. How are you?" She pulled her shirt over her head and tossed it aside.

I shrugged. "I'm not gonna cry over him because we didn't get that close." *Maybe.* "But I'm not wantin' to join everyone for dinner."

"There are other restaurants." She slipped a dress over her head, and I helped zipped the back for her. "I'm up for sushi if you're willin'."

"Well, we are on the sea, so my expectations are very high."

"Sushi it is," she said. "And if it's not good we can throw a fit like Josie."

I rolled my eyes. "I'll let her keep that role. Not me." I sighed. "You know, I was gonna pay for another excursion for the guys for Florence tomorrow. But now I think I just want our *us* time."

"I'm down with that."

"You won't be disappointed if you don't see Koa?"

"Nope. If you're okay with it, I was gonna meet up with him to dance later. Are you up for dancin'?"

I thought about it and thought of all the other men on the ship. There were a fair few who were good looking. Maybe not as chiseled and perfect as Preston, but still easy on the eyes. "You know what. I'll go dancin'. Count me in." *Maybe I'll stop hurting so much.*

Preston

I couldn't understand why I agreed to go dancing in the first place. Watching Billie sway in the arms of other men felt like a punch to the gut. I didn't know why it affected me so much, but I knew I couldn't stick around for more than an hour. I used the excuse of being tired to skip out on the night. Josie whined, but I didn't care. She even hinted not so subtly that she would come with me and even offered to give me a massage. I turned her down. No way did I want her paws on me.

She might have proof of Billie admitting she was a gold digger, but she should look in the mirror sometime.

The next day I didn't see Billie once. The guys and I went on our tour of Florence where we saw Michelangelo's statue of David. I even bought my mama an apron with the image of David's torso. She's gonna love it.

The next morning, we went off to tour Cannes, France. Unfortunately, Josie and her friends were on the same tour as us. The whole time she hung on me, never letting me enjoy a moment to stop alone and admire the views of the land and sea. The bus took us to a town called Frejus where I ate a baguette under a cork tree and toured an old medieval church. I found the history fascinating and would have liked to stay longer, but Josie complained and wanted me to take her outside to enjoy the shade.

"What do you think of the tour so far?" I asked Josie, hoping to take the continuing subject of shopping to something more interesting.

"We should have just gone shopping," she said and ran her hands up my chest, pressing into me. "Maybe one day you and I could travel to Paris together. I've always wanted to shop in Paris."

"I think you're getting ahead of—"

She cut me off by yanking me into her lips by my shirt. My lips didn't respond, nor did I guide her into me. It took me all of a few seconds to know that I didn't want this, so I stepped away, holding her back with wide eyes. She smiled coyly at me.

"Uh…" I glanced up to see the tour guide waving for us to follow. "It looks like the bus is leaving. We better go."

During the bus ride back, I had to fight with Josie to keep her hands to herself. She'd give me pouty lips and complain I was being too shy when she knew I wanted her. Each time I tried to explain that I wasn't into her like that, she would interrupt and prattle on about something she'd seen or heard.

I couldn't help but wish I could have Billie by my side instead, even if she was a gold digger. At least she was a shield. A fun shield. Each time I thought of her I tried to push her out of my mind. I thought I did a fairly good job of it, until the tour ended. As we were loading into small boats that took us back to the ship I ran into Ivory and Billie who were also waiting to load into a boat. I hadn't realized how much I'd been thinking about her until I saw her again. And, crap. It hurt to see her.

Koa was excited to meet up with them, so we ended up sitting together as a group. Josie made sure Billie noticed her hanging on me. I said hello to Billie to be civil and asked what they ended up seeing. My question caused Ivory to break out into a fit of giggles and Billie blushed excessively.

"What happened?" Koa asked. "You have to tell us now."

"We had no idea that the beach we decided to go to was clothing optional." Ivory laughed harder and Billie lowered in the seat.

"You're a bit shocked, Billie?" Koa asked, teasingly.

"You might say that," she answered.

"Figures," Josie smirked with her remark.

I couldn't help but laugh at how adorable Billie was about discovering a nude beach. She shot me a dirty look that instantly silenced me. Once we disembarked from the cruise ship, we parted ways with the ladies and headed to dinner. Josie's group was there, but not Billie or Ivory. Again. By the end of dinner, I was starting to wish Josie had kept me in the dark about Billie. Whether she was a gold digger or not, at least I would have had someone fun to talk to and dance with.

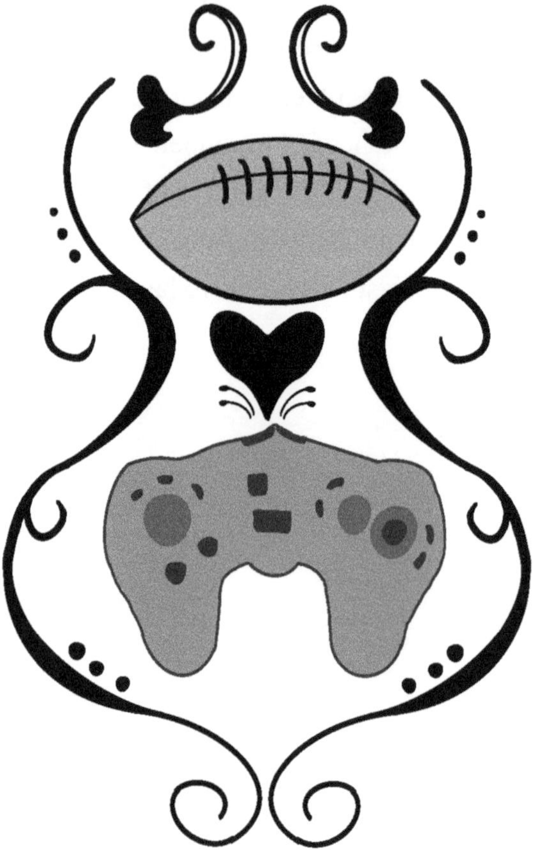

Nine

Billie

What do you call a group of gamers out in public? A rare occurrence.

Ivory waved at me to join her on the dance floor, but Koa was at her side and I didn't feel like being the third wheel. I shook my head, sipped my drink, and swayed a bit to the beat. Not for the first time I caught sight of Preston in the booth across the room. Josie was hanging on his arm and giggling excessively.

Preston glanced my way and momentarily locked eyes with me. I turned, wishing I hadn't been caught watching. I wasn't supposed to care. I had no claim on him.

"Hi. I've seen you here a time or two," a man, easy on the eyes, said and stepped up next to me. He brushed his dark hair back behind his ear and smiled at me. "What's your name?"

"Billie. And yours?" I asked, turning fully to him.

"Elton." He held his hand out for mine and surprised me by kissing it when I placed my hand in his. "Are you here alone?"

"Define alone."

He chuckled. "Do you have a boyfriend, husband, or significant other with you?"

"No." I smiled. "My friend Ivory and I are just havin' fun seein' this little part of the world."

"Let me guess, you're from either Tennessee or Texas."

"You're right on the last one." I took a sip of my drink as he grinned for having guessed right. "And you're from the northeast, given by your accent."

"You're good."

"Not that good. You guessed my state, but I guessed only your region."

"So, I've seen you dancing a few times earlier and I have to admit I've been hoping for a chance to dance with you. Would you?"

"Sure."

I had to give it to Elton. He knew how to dance, but his way of dancing was too close for comfort. Yes, I danced the same way with Preston, but that was … well, wanted. And we'd gotten to know each other a bit before dancing so close. Elton and I only had a short conversation, and he wanted his hands all over me.

At the end of two dances, I yelled to him over the music that I needed fresh air. I let Ivory know I was heading to my room then made my way to the door. I didn't know Elton had followed me out until I was in the elevator. "You didn't need to come with me. I'm just runnin' to my room for a minute to freshin' up." I told him.

"I'll go with you. I just thought we could talk without having to shout. Get to know each other a bit," he said, watching the teenagers that loaded into the elevator with us.

I smiled when I noticed the symbol of my company's gaming system across one of the teen's shirts. I shifted my attention to him. "What's your favorite game?" I gestured to his shirt after he gave me a funny look.

His smile grew big. "End of Havoc. I can't wait for the next one to come out."

"Me too." I winked and waved goodbye when I left the elevator.

"You like games?" Elton asked once we were alone.

"Yeah. You could say that." I slipped my keycard out of my bra, ready to open my door.

Elton slipped his arm around my waist, turning me to face him, then pressing me against my door. "I like to play games too."

What the heck!

The elevator down the hall dinged. When he went in for a kiss I dodged and caught a glimpse of the elevator doors opening. At the same time Elton's hands traveled up my ribs. "Get away from me!" I pushed him back with all my strength, but it only made him take a single step back.

"Come on, open your door." He growled and tried to come at me again, but my fist connected with his face, interrupting his progression.

"Hey! Get away from her!"

I glanced to see Preston sprinting toward us. Before Elton could attack again, I hurried into my room, shutting the door in his face. I pressed my body against it as if he might break down the door. I screamed at the sound of shouts right outside.

I slid down the door, digging my heels into the floor. My hand hurt and it took a moment to realize why. I'd punched someone. I'd had to do it before, but that was because a bully at middle school had dumped their food into my hair after teasing me about being flat chested and having ugly hair.

This time it was for a totally different reason. A reason I hoped never happened.

How could I have been so stupid? I should have stayed or asked for Ivory to go with me.

Pounding on my door startled me so bad I screamed and jumped.

"Billie. Are you okay?" Preston called through the door. When I didn't answer he continued. "I saw what happened, but I was too slow to reach you. Are you hurt?"

"I'm fine." Yeah. Like he'd believe that after a sob interrupted my words.

"Will you open the door?"

I shook my head, even though he couldn't see.

"Billie? Please, open the door."

I took a steadying breath and rose off the floor. "I'm fine. Don't worry about me."

"You're not fine. Open the door, Billie. The ships' police are coming, and you'll need to talk to them. Someone must have reported it."

"What? No! I'm fine. He didn't do anything," I called through the door. "He didn't even kiss me. I'm okay!" No. This can't be happening. My face and the whole horrid story will be plastered all over the news. I didn't want to be known for this. I didn't want the constant reminder. "Preston, go away. Tell them I'm fine and I don't want to talk about it. Don't tell them my name, or I'll hunt you down and tear out your liver and feed it to my dog."

"Billie, you can't let him get away with it."

"Then you tell them what you saw, but leave my name out of it." I opened the door so he could see how serious I was. His shoulders slumped as if relieved to see me. "Tell them he attacked someone, but I ran off, or whatever."

He pointed down the hall. "There are cameras. They likely saw it all and have found the guy. They'll know you're in here."

Great. I'm gonna have to get a hold of my lawyers and have them clean things up for me. Maybe they could get the ship's police to sign some kind of nondisclosure agreement.

"I'm fine. Don't you see that I'm not hurt?"

He held out his hand. "Give me your hand."

I held my aching hand behind me. "Just go." I slammed the door in his face, wishing he'd feel the same sting I had over the past few days. But for me, it was just a figurative door that had been slammed shut.

What a way to end the cruise.

Preston

The luggage behind me hit my ankle and I cursed under my breath. The glare the woman in the elevator gave me indicated that I hadn't said it quietly enough. She held her son closer to her.

"Sorry," I said, but I'd bet the young teen heard such words at school all the time.

The doors opened and we exited onto the lobby deck. Through the crowd I found Noah and Delany waiting. I gave them fist bumps and said hello. Seconds later Koa arrived with Ivory tucked under his arm. Behind them followed Billie. I said a quick greeting to the two then kept my gaze on Billie, trying to ascertain if she was okay.

She had sunglasses over her eyes, hiding any way for me to see if I should retreat or comfort. I went for comfort. "Hi. Are you okay?"

"Why would Billie not be okay?" Ivory asked me.

I shot a glance at Billie. She pressed her lips together. "I'm fine. Someone just tried to get fresh with me last night, but I punched him in the nose."

"What!" Ivory shrieked. "You didn't tell me? When did this happen?"

"Right after I left the club. But I'm fine."

"Where is the guy?" Noah asked with fists clenched. "I'd like to have a word or two with him."

"Please. Leave it be. If you make a big deal of it I'll tan your hide," Billie growled.

"But you're sure you're okay?" Delany asked at the same time Koa asked a similar question.

"I'm fine. He didn't hurt me, so we can all forget about it."

Right. Like I could. When everyone raised their phones to get the travel itinerary I placed a hand on Billie's shoulder. "I'm sorry I didn't get there sooner."

"It's fine," her words were clipped so I dropped the subject. For now.

"Hey, guys." Delany held up his phone. "All of the flights going in and out of Atlanta are grounded due to tornadoes. I guess a huge storm is going through, messing up flights all over the Midwest and some of the southern states."

"Is our flight canceled?" I asked.

"Not yet but it's not lookin' good," Delany answered.

"Coach will have our hide if we're not back on time." Koa pulled out his own phone. "I'll text him."

Ivory nudged Billie, but looked at Koa and I. "We'll take you home."

Noah laughed. "How ya gonna do that, angel? Got extra sets of wings?"

"Ivory," Billie grumbled a warning.

"What? It'll be fine. We have room."

They shared a few looks with each other, then Ivory whispered in her ear.

"Fine," Billie said, then lifted her phone to her ear.

"What's that all about?" Koa asked with a chuckle.

Ivory smiled. "Part of this honeymoon gift my relative gave me came with a private jet ride home. I'm inviting y'all to ride home with us. We can avoid the storm and fly straight home instead of having any layovers."

"Sweet!" Noah slapped Ivory's hand. "She's our good luck charm, guys."

I wanted to ask why Billie needed to give the go-ahead. Was Billie related to whoever gave Ivory the gift? And why did it sound like Billie was making the arrangements?

I didn't get the chance to ask since she avoided us by claiming the need to use the restroom.

Thirty minutes later Billie announced that our ride to the airport had arrived. As we were leaving, I heard my name called. I tried not to visibly shrink away when Josie came at me to give me a hug.

She leaned away but hung onto my neck. "You'll call me, won't you?"

"Um. Josie, you're nice and all, but..."

She frowned. "What? I thought you liked me."

"Sorry. But we're not compatible. I've been trying to say that for days now." I pulled her arms from around my neck. "Safe travels." I nodded to Mallory and Trisha. "Bye, ladies." I glanced to my left and saw the group had already started down the gangplank. I turned to leave but Josie's hand dug into my arm.

"Does this have anything to do with Billie? You know she was using you, right? You should have heard the terrible things she said about you."

"She has nothing to do with it. Goodbye, Josie. Don't call me." I tugged my arm free and hurried away, hoping she didn't follow right behind me. I caught up to the group as they were loading into a shuttle van.

Billie sat shotgun and chatted with the driver about Spain and if he liked living there. I used the time to flip through my photos I took and erase the ones that were no good. We arrived at the airport and went through all the protocols, which was far different from commercial flights. The private jet sat waiting for us on the tarmac. I found it odd that Billie greeted a woman wearing a business suit waiting at the foot of the stairs leading up to the jet. I was too far away to hear what they talked about, but it looked like the woman was going over some kind of list on her tablet.

My jaw dropped as we stepped onto the plane. Right at the entrance, a couple of tables surrounded by plush leather seats greeted us. As we moved further in, I spotted a bar tucked away in the corner.

The woman who greeted us smiled and pointed out the room. "You're welcome to help yourself to the bar and there is a full bathroom at the back next to the bedroom. Let me know if you'd like a blanket and pillow. We'll have meals prepared for you whenever you're ready."

Billie disappeared through the bedroom door. Before she closed the door she stuck her head out. "Candace, can I speak to you when you're finished helping them?"

"Sure thing," the hostess answered.

I found a seat beside Noah after stowing away my luggage. "This is going to spoil me and I'll never want to fly commercial again," I said to Noah.

"No kiddin," he answered. "I get the feeling like Billie knows her way around this jet like she owns the place. Do you think there's more to her than what she seems?"

I shrugged. "Ivory said it was a relative. They probably flew here on this jet and she's just a little more familiar than we are."

"Maybe." Noah pushed a button on his chair and the legs moved out. "Oh. I want a jet now." Another woman walked by who acted the part of a stewardess. Noah nodded at her with a smile. Once she passed he leaned in. "She's hot. Do you think she's single?"

I rolled my eyes.

Billie returned, taking a chair at the table and buckling in. Candace sat beside her and buckled as well. Ten minutes later we were shoved back into our seats as we rose into the sky. Once we leveled off, I watched as Billie and Candace talked over tablets as though they were working. Billie raised a remote to the wall at the front of the plane and clicked a button. A TV rose from a side table. One of the games she had played earlier this week loaded on the screen and she began playing.

A huge part of me wanted to go join her and ask to play, but she'd given every indication she didn't want anything to do with me.

The long flight continued with a couple of meals and naps here and there. Billie stayed distant and spent most of her time in a room, probably sleeping. I had a hard time sleeping so I drank several shots of liquor to help knock me out. Probably too many shots. We arrived in Dallas late in the afternoon, but this time we taxied up to a terminal and exited into the airport. The effects of the alcohol hadn't worn off yet, so I swayed, bumping into Koa.

Koa shook his head, grinning at me. "You know, whoever this relative is of Ivory's I hope I get to meet him and become friends, because I don't ever want to fly commercial again."

I laughed. "You and me both."

"You okay?" Koa asked.

I laughed. "Just a bit drunk still. It'll go away soon. Do you want to share an Uber?"

"No need for that," Ivory said and fell into step next to me. "We've already arranged for a ride."

"Wow! Gold star treatment to the max!" Koa pulled Ivory into his arm and kissed the side of her head. She gave him a nervous smile.

"Are you sure?" I asked, watching Billie walking ahead of us.

She does have a nice sway to her perfect hips. I laughed, still feeling a bit off in the head. I really shouldn't have had that much to drink. My head felt muddledee. Muddlerer. Muderd. Whatever.

"Of course," Ivory said. Just follow Billie.

A man just outside of the security barrier ran to Billie, pulling her into a hug. He had the same red, flaming hair and facial features and didn't look much younger than Billie. She kissed his cheek then wiped the lipstick off of him. When I closed the distance between us we all grouped together. Billie waved to the man. "This is my brother, Malcolm. Malcolm, this is Noah, Koa, Delany, and Preston."

Malcolm's eyes grew big. He slugged Billie on the arm playfully. "You brought home the Nighthawks? And you didn't say anything about it? Wait." He narrowed his eyes on her. "Did you even know who these fellas are?"

"She didn't at first." Ivory laughed.

"Shut up," Billie grumbled when her brother laughed, too.

"Well, that's not a surprise. It's nice to meet y'all." He shook our hands, and we greeted him with smiles. "Well, the van's straight out through that door beyond the pickup line. We better hurry before I get a parking ticket." Malcolm grabbed one of Ivory's bags and led the way.

A couple of teenagers rushed up to Billie, holding out pads of paper, as if asking for something. She stopped and let go of her suitcase. The carry-on toppled over so I stopped to help.

"What is your favorite game?" Billie asked and wrote something on the pad offered to her. Everyone else continued on. The boys rushed to answer. I adjusted my shoulder bag and held the two suitcases, trying to figure out what was going on.

She finished a minute later then turned to see me waiting. Her smile faded. "Thanks. I'll take it." She took the carry-on and we both headed toward the door. The second we exited, a large group of people rushed us, holding phones, microphones, and cameras in our faces. Questions were shouted at us.

"Miss Leigh! Are you excited to be a billionaire?"

"What are your future plans for Legions Gaming?"

"You just came from a honeymoon cruise trip. Does this mean you're married? Is this your new husband?"

"I understand you have a baby girl. Can you tell us about her?"

One man shoved a camera in my face. "Aren't you the quarterback for the Nighthawks?"

"When did you get married?"

"Is this your wife?"

I laughed and put my arm on Billie's shoulder. "Yeah, right." I slurred sarcastically. "Billie and I are married."

"What?" Billie's eyes got big before they narrowed. She pushed through the crowd, grabbing my hand with her free one and yanked me with her. "No comment!"

More questions were shouted as we pushed passed. All of it sounded confusing and muddled. We reached the van and Billie shouted at her brother. "Malcolm! We have to go fast!"

We piled in quickly, shutting the door before the arms holding microphones reached in. Billie held her hands over her face and cussed multiple times.

"What was that all about?" Noah asked from the back seat.

Ivory shot concerned glances between Billie and me. Malcolm drove as quickly as legally possible out of the airport.

"Did they say something about you being a billionaire?" Delany asked.

Billie sighed. "Yes. While on my cruise I earned my first billion. I am the creator and CEO of Legion Gaming."

Say what?

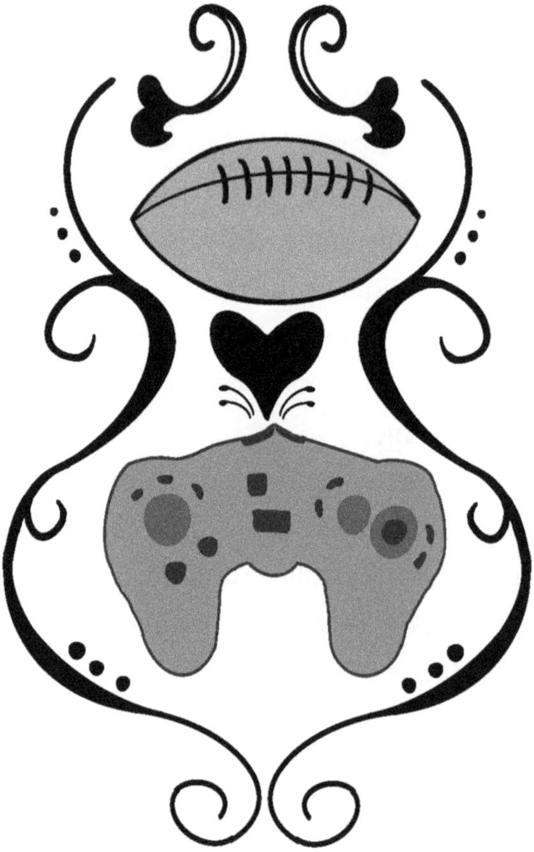

Ten

Billie

Two crabs are eating a billionaire on the bottom of the ocean. One looks at the other and asks, "Does this taste a little rich to you?"

The men around me cussed with disbelief. Preston stared at me, jaw slack.

"So, that was *your* private jet?" Noah asked.

"Yes." I sunk lower in my seat, wishing I could hide in the crack of the cushion and wallow among the crumbs and hardened gummy bears.

"You own a jet?" Koa asked in bewilderment. "Why didn't you tell us who you were?"

"Guys." Ivory shifted to face the men. "Billie didn't want people to know because it can be dangerous for people to know who she is and how much she's worth. Don't be upset. She has good reasons to keep her secrets."

"They found out about Cas," I said to Ivory. "They asked about her."

"Great," both Ivory and Malcolm muttered.

"And they thought Preston and I were married." I waved at him next to me.

"Wait! What?" Everyone in the van asked at the same time.

"Why would they think that?" Ivory asked.

"They mentioned something about a honeymoon trip. Someone must have found out I booked a honeymoon suite package and assumed I'd gotten married. And then genius here," I waved at Preston, "practically confirmed it when they asked if we were married."

"What?" Everyone yelled again. Noah slapped Preston on the back of the head.

"What? No, I didn't," Preston protested. "I thought it was funny and was being sarcastic."

"You really shouldn't have drunk anything, man," Koa said to Preston.

"Sorry! I didn't know!" Preston threw his hands up.

"You'll just have to set them straight," Malcolm said from the driver seat while glancing in the mirror at me.

"Yeah. That will be fun," I grumbled and ran my fingers through my hair.

"Who's Cas?" Koa asked, leaning forward from the back seat.

I sighed. "She's my daughter."

"What?" the men asked in unison.

"I have an eleven-month-old baby girl," I answered, then got funny looks from the men. "Look. I don't want to talk about this right now. I need to do some damage control with my assistant." I turned forward and started texting Candace to ask for help and let her know what happened. She responded that she'd look into it. A few minutes later she sent me a text with a link.

This doesn't look good. Evidently, you're married now. How did that happen?

I clicked on the link to a website filled with pics of Preston and I exiting the airport. The largest and most dominant one was Preston's arm over my shoulder and a dopey smile on his face. I of course looked drunk or as if someone had knocked me upside the head seconds before.

I frowned and called her, trying to talk as quietly as I could to explain what happened. Preston received a call of his own, and by the few words I caught he too was questioned about our marital status.

"Listen," Candace said to me over the phone. "This doesn't look good. Preston's remark sounds a little sarcastic, but it really does sound like he's claimed you as his wife. I don't know how to help you fix this without it affecting your company. People don't like being tricked or lied to and it *will* affect your revenue."

"What?" Preston yelled into his phone beside me. "You can't be serious!" A few choice words growled out between his teeth.

"Would you like me to call a meeting with the board?" Candace asked through the phone.

"Yeah. Set it up for first thing tomorrow morning," I responded, rubbing the bridge of my nose. A headache was coming on and all I wanted to do was cuddle my baby and take a nap.

"Maybe sooner would be better," Candace said, sounding unsure.

"I can't join today, but if they need to meet, they can do it without me for now. It can wait."

A minute later, after hanging up with Candace, I locked eyes with Ivory. Her gaze conveyed her apologies and concern for me—no words were necessary.

"So, is this a bad time to tell you that there's a surprise waiting for you at home?" Malcolm asked and glanced at me in the mirror.

"I don't know if I can handle another surprise," I answered.

"Well, this one will go away, and you'll miss out." When I didn't respond he continued. "Emmett is at home, waiting to see you, but he flies out in about an hour."

Ivory sat taller. "Emmett is in town?"

Preston

"What!" Billie sat forward at the news that some man was waiting at her house. "He's here?"

All I could do was stare at my phone after hanging up with my agent and my PR. I was in shock.

"He's been here for a couple of days. He didn't want us to say anything because he wanted to surprise you." Malcolm went on, but I tuned him out.

What did they mean they wanted me to be married? Did they really think they couldn't fix this?

Noah's hand clamped down on my shoulder. "Spill it. What did they say?"

"They want me to get married." I swallowed hard. "They said that if I go back on what I said then I'll be hated, shunned by fans. And if it got bad enough, they'd drop me."

"That's ridiculous," Koa said, but my attention was drawn to Billie's narrowed gaze piercing me.

"What do you mean?" she asked through thin lips.

"They said that if I retract my statement about us being married my fans' disappointment will affect the sales of tickets. My career will be affected by this." I rubbed my hand down my face and sighed. "This is ridiculous."

"I am meeting with my board of directors tomorrow morning

at eight. I want you," she pointed at me, "there with your public relations rep. We need to figure this out."

"I have practice in the morning."

"You'll have to skip it. You got me into this mess, so you're gonna get us out," she said then twisted forward and folded her arms.

"Me?" I pressed a hand against my chest then waved at her. "You're the one that's all loaded with money that caused the press to be waiting at the door. I had nothing to do with it."

She shot me a look that could kill. "You were the one who grinned like an idiot and practically confirmed we were married."

I huffed and folded my arms, staring out the window. The city had started giving way to the suburban neighborhoods, but my attention wasn't on the world around me. All I could think of was what this would mean for my career.

Billie turned to the men behind me. "Do y'all mind if I get dropped off first? My brother whom I haven't seen in over a year is there and he won't be for very long. And I'm not sure when I'll get to see him next. Malcom can take y'all home after."

"No problem," Noah said. "Would it be okay if I used your toilet?"

"Yeah. I'm pretty sure my family will want to meet y'all anyway," Billie said, glancing at me.

"Yeah, mom and dad will especially want to meet your new husband." Malcolm's comment earned him a slap on the back of the head by Billie.

New husband. This day just kept getting worse. None of it would have happened had I not lingered behind to be a gentleman and help Billie with her luggage. And if she had been more honest from the start.

She's a billionaire! And a mom! And apparently a liar. Me and the guys were led to believe she was this virtuous virgin—a financially struggling virtuous virgin living in her parents' basement.

When we entered a gated community I knew well, I shook my head. Great. She lives close to me. The van slowed as we neared the end of a cul-de-sac where a large iron and wood gate divided the road from a giant house beyond. Billie cursed at seeing all of the press standing at the gate and waiting. Video cameras pointed at the van as we neared. Malcolm pressed a button on the visor and the gate opened. Thankfully, the press hung back as we drove through. The long drive through the trees and perfectly trimmed bushes screamed money. The stone house with arched windows gave me pause. This wasn't out of my own price range, but this whole time when I pictured Billie's home, I expected a simple house with a tire swing in the front and several beat up cars in the driveway.

This was far from that image.

"How did they find out where we lived?" Malcolm asked.

"Were they here when you left?" Billie asked him.

"No."

The moment the van door opened a man came charging out of the house with arms wide. His military haircut told me it was Billie's brother. He didn't have blazing red hair, his was brown, but his features were similar. Billie pushed past me and hurried to give him a hug. She kissed his cheek repeatedly, and I heard her crying as she spoke in his ear.

When the man saw me step out from the van he grinned. "So, you went and married Preston Kyler! And didn't invite me to the weddin'?"

"When did you hear about it?" Malcolm asked.

"Like two minutes ago. Dad noticed the press at the front door and checked the internet to figure it out," he answered. "They're none too pleased to hear you up and got hitched without tellin' them."

Billie slugged him in the shoulder. "The press got it all wrong and assumed we're married."

"Seriously?" he laughed then held his hand out to me. "I'm Emmett. Billie's more handsome brother."

"He ain't lyin'." Ivory stepped from behind Koa.

"Ivory." Emmitt's eyes grew big and looked her over. "You're all grown up."

"It's been a while," she said as he pulled her into a hug then gave her another once over before shaking hands with the rest of the group.

"Well, enough yappin'. Let's go inside." Malcolm waved everyone to follow, and we all entered.

The entryway and great room were filled with rustic Asian furniture. Large, antique-looking paintings adorned every open wall, while decorative Asian carvings nestled in the corners and on tables. Had she traveled to Thailand to acquire all of this decor?

Four adults stood from their seats in the living room when we entered. Billie hugged the man I assumed was her father first. "Hi, Daddy. How are you feelin'?"

"Fine, fine." He shook his head as if irritated that she would ask. "What's this about you getting married?"

"False alarm, Dad," Malcolm said and plopped down on the couch. "The press assumed she did because she was on a honeymoon cruise."

"It's all a huge misunderstanding that I hope to fix tomorrow with the board," Billie said. "Where's my baby?"

"Sleeping. She should be awake by now," the woman now hugging Billie said.

Billie waved to the group. "Mom, Dad. This is Preston Kyler, Koa—"

"You don't have to tell us who they are, honey," her dad said.

"We already know."

"Well, this is my dad and mom, Nathan and Daisy. And this," she waved at the other couple, "is my brother and sister-in-law, Gage and Karli. And their cute little baby." Gage looked lankier than her younger brothers. Emmett was twice his size.

We all greeted each other with handshakes and waves. A noticeable change came over Billie; she seemed at peace and genuinely happy with her family nearby, as if this was where she truly belonged.

"My parents live in the cottage out back, and Gage and Karli live about thirty minutes away. But they're here a few times a week at least. And Malcolm lives in the cottage too—at least for now," Billie said as though she were trying to shove him out the door. "The only one away from home is Emmett." She put her arm around Emmett and held him like he'd suddenly vanish into thin air, and she'd never see him again.

"Hey, I found a dorm room, so I'll be moving out when school starts." Malcolm raised his hands in defense.

"I don't mean to break up the reunion, but can I use your restroom?" Noah asked.

While Noah was shown to a restroom Billie disappeared down a hall. I chatted with her family for a time and they asked about the Nighthawks' stats. "Y'all should come to our first home game in a month," I said. "In fact, I'll get you tickets."

"You don't have to do that." Daisy waved her hand as if batting away the idea.

"It's the least we can do for Billie for getting us home in time," Delany said then glanced at his watch.

"Dad." Malcolm looked at his father pointedly. "Don't you dare turn them down."

I laughed. "I'll take care of everything."

Noah joined us in the room. "Well, we should probably be going."

"We can call an uber, so you don't have to go driving us around," I said then pulled my phone out as it started to ring.

"Nonsense. Malcolm and I can take you," Nathan said and went to the closet for what I assumed were his shoes.

I answered the phone and stepped toward the entry. "Yeah?"

"Hey, Preston. Where are you now? Can we meet and talk about this marriage fiasco?" Henry, my PR rep asked.

"I'm at Billie's house right now," I answered and watched Billie enter with a child in her arms. A child that was obviously not blood-related, given how dark her skin was. My curiosity piqued but I had a call to my ear. I peered out the front window, only to see even more press standing around beyond the gate. "We're about to leave—that is, if we can get past the press out front."

"You can't leave," he said.

"What do you mean? Why not?"

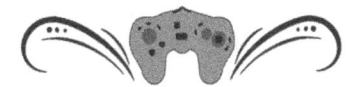

Billie

"Everyone, this is Cassidy—or Cas for short. She's my sweet little baby."

"Well, I can't say she looks like her mom, cuz I'd be lyin'." Delany laughed and waved at Cas, wiggling the ends of his fingers. His tuff guy demeanor softened instantly at the sight of her.

"Yeah. It's no secret she's adopted," I said and snuggled her into my chest. Oh, I missed her softness and her baby smell. I never want to leave her again. It was torture. Her little hands clung to my shirt as she rubbed her sleepy face into my chest.

"She's my sister's baby," Ivory said. "She's named after her."

"Cassidy and I were best friends growing up. And nearly two years ago Cas got pregnant. She never figured out who the father was. Still don't know." I kissed her cheek and emotion crept up my throat. "Cas died giving birth and I just couldn't let this part of Cas go."

Ivory crossed the room and brushed Cas's hair with her long nails. "I would have taken her, but I wasn't in a good place when she was born. But Billie is family to me." She smiled at me with tears in her eyes.

"She's beautiful," Preston whispered from the entry, his attention on Cas. He ran his fingers through his hair, swallowing hard and looking a little ill.

"Dude. Are you okay?" Noah asked.

"Uh. Can I talk to you for a minute, Billie?" he asked.

I nodded and carried Cas with me, not wanting to let go of her. I led the way into the front formal room and sat on the sofa. "What's wrong? Other than everyone thinkin' we're married?" I couldn't help the ice in my tone.

He lowered himself in the chair diagonally from me. "Um. I don't know how to say this. But ... Everyone thinks we're married."

"Yeah. I know that part."

"Well, now everyone knows I'm here at your house." He pointed with his thumb out of the front window. *More press. Great.* The sun hung low in the sky and soon they'd be able to see in once the indoor lights were on.

I closed my eyes before hitting him with a death glare. "Perfect," I grumbled.

"Which means, if I leave, people will speculate and question why. They'll think I'm leaving you."

"Then leave."

"But then it will damage our public images. My career will

suffer and I'm assuming your company's image."

I sighed. "Perfect," I said again.

"I've been advised to stay here. At least until we can figure this out."

"Like, as in spend the night?" I asked.

"Yeah."

I sighed again.

"I've also been told the press are waiting at my house in case we show up there. If I show up there alone then people will wonder what's going on."

I pressed my lips together, wanting to chew him out for flappin' his gums at the airport.

"Look." He leaned forward and rested his elbow on his knee. "I'm really sorry about this. I didn't mean for this to happen."

Keep your apology and shove it. "Come on. I'll show you to my guest room." I stood and held Cas close. She clung like she didn't want to let me go as much as I didn't want to let her go. She started gabbin' nonsense as I headed back into the great room.

"You ready to go, man?" Noah asked Preston.

"I'll be stayin'." Preston went on to explain the reasoning for it. My parents only stood there with wide eyes and didn't speak a word.

Koa and Noah chuckled as if it were all a joke which earned a slug from Preston. Koa, Noah, and Delany gave me a hug goodbye with promises to keep in touch.

"I have to be going, too. Is someone willin' to drop me off at the airport?" Emmett asked. He was now dressed in his army garb, complete with hat. His duffle was slung over his shoulder.

"Malcolm and Dad can drop me off at home first to get my car then I can take you," Ivory offered.

His smile widened. "Sounds perfect."

For ten minutes, I shared a tearful goodbye with my brother and exchanged quick farewells with the guys and Ivory. I waved from inside the house, ensuring the press couldn't catch a glimpse of us. The moment the doors closed all eyes turned to both me and Preston.

"I owe y'all an apology. I'm sorry this mess has happened," Preston said to mostly my mom and oldest brother.

"Well, what's done is done. No use cryin' over spilt milk." Mama waved us into the kitchen. "There's soup in the slow cooker and I made bread."

"You're the best, Mama." I kissed her cheek. Cas grunted and pressed into me more.

Mom laughed. "I get the feelin' she's not gonna wanna let you go now that you're home."

"I'm fine with that. I wish I could take her with me to work tomorrow." I glanced at Preston who chatted with Gage and Karli. "I better go show him the guest room."

"Are you sure you want him stayin' in here?" Mama asked. "We've been stayin' in your room while you were gone since it's closest to Cas. We planned to head back into the cottage tonight, but if you want someone close, Dad and I can stay in the second guest room."

"No. It's okay. I trust him. And it's not like we're happy with each other right now. He was kinda a jerk the last two days."

"Are you sure you can trust a jerk?" she asked.

"He's not a jerk. He just acted like one." *Maybe.*

Eleven

Preston

"To keep your marriage brimming with love in the wedding cup, whenever you're wrong, admit it; whenever you're right, shut up." —Ogden Nash

I blew on the spoonful of beef and veggie soup before taking the bite, chewing, and letting it slide down my throat. "This is delicious, Mrs. Leigh."

"I didn't make it. I found a container of it frozen in the freezer," she answered. I followed her gaze to Billie.

Billie's cheeks pinked. "I like to do freezer meals."

I smiled. I liked a woman who could cook. The more I learned the more I realized I'd misjudged her completely. Guilt tugged at me again. What a jerk I'd been. A billionaire. Crazy that I thought she'd be a gold digger. "You're a very good cook."

"Thanks," she responded without a glance my way. Her attention was drawn to Cas in her highchair who was taking it upon herself to throw every pea to the floor. "No, baby. You're supposed to eat them."

Billie's older brother and his wife had left before eating, with the excuse that they had a dinner date planned with friends. Before they left, Billie had them swear to keep the whole marriage mess a secret. They agreed and left, calling later to notify us that even more press were at the house.

Daisy and I shared small talk while Billie occupied herself with Cas. Nathan and Malcolm soon returned home and joined us in the kitchen. "Oh, no!" Malcolm called when he neared his niece. "Cas peed on the floor!"

I was confused for a moment until I remembered the pile of sweet peas that Cas had thrown down. I chuckled and Billie rolled her eyes. "You're so childish."

Nathan slapped his son's shoulder. "Good one, son. You'll have the dad jokes down to perfection by the time you have kids of your own."

Malcolm nudged my arm as I was lifting my spoon to my lips. A carrot plopped off and back into my bowl. He shot me an apologetic look then cleared his throat. "Hey, Preston. Do you think sometime soon we can toss a football around?"

I smiled and noticed Billie glancing at me with a not so favorable glower. "Uh, sure. I'd like that." I was surprised to know that my words were true. In the short time that I interacted with Billie's family I found I liked them and could see myself getting along with them. That was unless Billie didn't behead me first.

"Right on. Right now the skeeters are out and will eat us alive, but maybe tomorrow?" he asked.

"I'll see what I've got goin' on."

"Well, she's done eating." Billie stood and grabbed a washcloth from her mama and started cleaning Cas up. Her adorable brown cheeks puffed up in protest from being harassed by her mother. She screeched and pushed the towel away. Billie changed tactics by singing a playful song and going in for quick wipes as if it were a game. Cas giggled but still protested the cleaning.

"You're good with babies," I said to Billie.

"She babysat all through middle school, so she had lots of practice," Daisy said then held out her hand to me. "Are you finished, or do you want seconds?"

I smiled, loving the home cooked meal. A man could get used to this. "How about thirds?"

She laughed and filled my bowl up for me.

"So, what do you do for a living?" I asked Nathan.

"I am a track coach at the high school, and I teach math and computer science. I used to teach in Texas, but when Billie started her business here, we had to move to be close."

"That's why all of his kids were on the track team. Dad wouldn't let us bow out on being a part of the team," Malcolm said around a mouthful of bread.

We chatted more about coaching and sports as we all sat around the table, and I ate through my fourth serving of soup and homemade bread. Cas sat on her mom's lap until she pushed away to get down and play on the floor.

"So, tell us how you met?" Nathan asked before taking a bite of his sliced bread.

I glanced at Billie, ready for her to share the story so she could decide how much to reveal to her family. She took a deep breath, as if recalling it caused her pain. "I met all the guys on the first day aboard ship. We talked for a while and got along great so we all kinda just started hanging out together."

"And how did the whole marriage thing come into play?" Daisy asked.

"That's a case of being in the wrong place at the wrong time and my sarcasm getting me into trouble," I answered.

Billie went on to explain it better than I did. My phone rang so I excused myself to answer the call from my mother. My heart pounded, not wanting to answer, but I sucked it up anyway. What is she gonna say about this?

"Honey! I can't believe it! You're married? When did this happen? Why didn't you tell me?"

"Mama it's not—"

"Oh, honey! She's beautiful!"

"Mom I—"

"Now you don't have to worry about someone marrying you for your money because she's even richer than you!"

"There's something—"

"I always knew you'd catch a beautiful woman—she's much better than that Cassidee woman you were with. When are you gonna bring her by? We have to meet her!"

"Mom, it's—"

"You have to come for a visit. I'll never forgive you if you don't. We'll have a big ol' shindig. I've told every one of my friends and they all agree that they want to meet her."

In that moment, I realized I couldn't utter a word of the truth to my mama. If I did, it wouldn't be long before all of Texas found out. "I'll bring her by soon. I'll be a bit busy getting things settled. I'll talk to you soon. Bye, Mama." I hung up before she took another breath to carry on.

When I returned to the kitchen, I held up my phone. "That was my mama."

"Did you tell her the truth?" Billie asked.

I shook my head. "No. All of Texas would know if I told her. She has a lot of friends who get excited about me since I'm a quarterback and all."

Daisy nodded in understanding and Nathan grunted like a father would. The meal ended and I offered to help in the kitchen but was shooed out. We gathered in the family room and talked some more about the trip while Cas played with her mama on the floor. I couldn't help but admire her the more I watched her with her daughter. All the reasons I had for keeping her at arm's length suddenly faded away, and I found myself wishing I could rewind to the time before I messed everything up.

I'm a fool. I owed her more apologies than any one man should.

"Uh, can I talk with you before we turn in tonight?" I asked Billie when her family was preoccupied debating about some family event in the past.

Before she could answer, Daisy stood. "We should be heading back to the cottage anyway. It's getting late. Unless you want help putting Cas to bed."

"No. I haven't been with Cas for over a week now. No way am I missin' a moment," Billie answered and growled into Cas's neck, tickling her.

"I figured you'd say that." Daisy waved at her husband and son, who followed her obediently after wishing us a goodnight. The back sliding door shut behind them and I watched their retreating figures head to a one-story house near the back in the trees.

"You have a great family," I said, lowering myself to the floor to hold one of the blocks out to Cas. She crawled over to me and took the block, giving me a once over. Probably questioning if she could trust me.

"I know. They're the best." She smiled. "Most of the time." I hadn't seen her smile in a few days and I realized then how much I'd missed it.

"I owe you many apologies."

Billie huffed.

I rested my elbow on my bent knee and leaned against the couch. "I'm sorry for being rude."

She lifted her brows at me as if urging me on.

"I was told by Josie that she overheard you talking about finding a rich husband or something, and that money mattered to you more than anything else."

"What?" Billie sat taller. "Why would she say that?"

"Trisha confirmed that she heard you say it."

Billie's lips pressed together, and her brows furrowed. "She might have heard me say something like that when I was complaining to Ivory about other people wanting to marry people for their money. It might have come off as me saying that I was looking for that. But as you can see," she waved around us, "a rich husband is not what I'm lookin' for, nor do I need one."

She stood and picked up Cas. I stood to follow her. "I realize you're not a gold digger now," I said.

"*Now*," she scoffed.

I grabbed my suitcase in the entry then followed her down a hall. "I'm really sorry for how I treated you." She walked into a room that was obviously a nursery. Soft purple and white decor filled the room with splashes of pinks. I rubbed the back of my head, hating how bad I was at apologizing. "I shouldn't have believed Josie."

"Nobody should believe Josie. She has horns holdin' up her halo." Billie laid Cas down on the changing table and started stripping her down.

I leaned against the wall at the foot of the changing table so I could face Billie without directly looking at Cas. "I should have talked to you about it instead of ignoring you."

"Yes, you should have," she said then leaned in to blow on Cas's belly. Cas giggled with delight.

Out of the corner of my eye, I saw Billie shaking powder onto Cas. A second later, I heard a loud fart, and Billie burst into laughter. I glanced down to see a puff of white powder resting on my arm, making the hair stand out more. "Did she just fart powder on me?"

"Yes. And it was quite impressive. I guess she showed you what she thinks of you and your apologies. Good girl, Cas."

I chuckled softly, but my heart sank further. She wasn't accepting my apologies.

Billie continued dressing Cas while I stood there silently pondering on what more I needed to say to get Billie back to being my friend again.

"There, all done and ready for bed." Billie lifted her into her arms and kissed her cheek. "Say goodnight to Preston."

"Goodnight, gorgeous." I lifted Cas's hand to my lips and kissed her little chubby fingers. She grunted and bounced at the same time, but didn't take her eyes from me. I grunted back in the same way. She grunted again, her body moving up and down. I grunted a bit lower. She giggled and grunted. We went back and forth until Cas rubbed her tired eyes.

"Wave goodnight." Billie waved to show her how it's done. Cas only grunted. "One day you'll get the waving thing down," she said and peppered her with kisses.

I meandered to the door and watched Billie lower her into a crib and place the blanket over her. Cas started to cry and Billie told her to go to sleep. She hurried to me and practically pushed me out of the room, closing the door behind us. She held her fingers to her lips then waved for me to follow her. Across the hall she paused at a set of open double doors. She kicked her shoes off into the room that I assumed was her room. She waved for me to follow again. Two doors down around the corner she opened a door.

"This is the guest room you can stay in. Hopefully it's for only one night." She pointed at a door to the right. "That's your private bathroom. There should be everything you need in there. If not, let me know."

Before she could walk away, I stopped her by taking her arm

gently. "Billie. I'm not done tellin' you I'm sorry."

She sighed and didn't look at me.

"I'm sorry for being a jerk. I'm sorry for not talking to you when I should have. And I'm really sorry I got you into a mess that might harm your business."

"Well. Hopefully it doesn't. Goodnight, Preston. We can drive together in the morning to my meeting then I'll have a car take you wherever you need to go after that."

She walked away and I said goodnight to her retreating back.

This wasn't gonna be easy to fix.

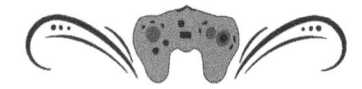

Billie

Shock washed over me. I sank into my office chair in the conference room, my jaw hanging open. For over an hour I had argued, trying to dismiss the facts. We examined every angle of what had been said in the media and the fact that our stocks were skyrocketing. The board *and* those present from the NFL Nighthawks' team all agreed—whether I agreed or not—that the best course of action was to get married.

For reals.

"Don't worry," they said. "It will only be for a short time. After the spotlight is off you and no one cares anymore you can get your marriage annulled."

How easy for them to say. It wasn't their life to mess with. Didn't marriage hold any weight to anyone these days?

Besides getting slapped in the face at their conclusion I had to sit while they read the comments and articles that were said about us. And my Cas. Hearing what they thought of my adoption hurt the worst. There was so much mud flung at me for adopting without a husband. Like that was a bad thing.

But Cas was my sister's baby. Not a blood sister, but a sister nonetheless and she chose me. Didn't people understand that it didn't matter? I love her and that was all that mattered. And who cares if I was single when I adopted her?

But now that I was "married" some people accept her as my own. How ridiculous. Like I had to have their approval.

"Hey." Preston lowered himself in front of me, breaking through my thoughts. I locked eyes with him. Could I do this? Could I marry this man? For the good of my company and for his career?

Preston took my hand in his and tried to smile but failed. "It will work out in the end. It will only last as long as you want it to—once the media dies down, of course."

I pulled my hand away. "This is all ridiculous."

"I know. But the sooner we take care of the loose ends the better." He stood, held out his hand to me. My gaze shifted to Candace who stood by the door. Everyone else had filed out. "So, what next?" I asked her, ignoring Preston's outstretched hand.

"You'll both need to fill out a marriage license online on the way to the courthouse," Candace answered. "Arizona law allows you to get married right away."

I stood and Preston rested his hand at my back as if to guide me to my office. I shook his hand off and stepped away from him. This was his fault.

Mike, my COO, caught my reaction when he reentered the room. He frowned. "You need to make the marriage believable. Act like you like him."

I glared at him and sighed. "Fine. But only in public."

"Fine by me." Mike shrugged. "Good luck and make sure people don't recognize you at the courthouse. You're already supposed to be married, remember."

As we approached to exit my building in Scottsdale, I saw the swarm of reporters and cameras through the glass. Preston's hand took hold of mine, and I almost pulled away, but remembered we had a show to put on. I didn't want my smile forced, so I thought of Cas and how cute she is. It helped the smiles stick. Lights flashed and questions were flung at me from every side. We made our way to the van that one of my employees had brought out of the parking garage.

We could have easily avoided the mess of reporters by heading straight to the garage, but the board insisted I show my face. When they asked what we were doing—which felt like a stupid question—I replied, "I was just showing Preston around the place."

"Will Preston be taking over the company at any point in the future?" one reporter asked.

I huffed out a laugh. *As if.* "No. Excuse us. We need to get through."

I slid into the driver's seat and pulled away with Preston at my side and Candace in the back. I grumbled a bit at the stupidity of the question I'd just heard. I drove like a bat out of hell around the city, trying to ditch the reporters that followed. My foul mood helped me to be a more aggressive driver. Preston gasped a few times when I weaved in and out of traffic. We had to take a long detour then backtrack to the courthouse. By the time we arrived I was livid but had to hide it.

We finished the forms online in the waiting room of the courthouse. I didn't notify my family what the verdict was, still hoping we'd be able to get out of it somehow. I believe he did the same, not saying a word to his friends or family. If I had to get married, I didn't want my family there to witness the humiliation. Especially if it drew attention to us. It wasn't like this was special anyway.

The clock on the wall ticked and I clung to my phone, praying someone would call and tell us it was all a joke, and I could go home single. The call didn't come. Preston eased the hat down further when someone glanced our way. Hopefully, our dark glasses and hats hid our identities enough that reporters wouldn't jump on us the second we exited the courthouse.

The advice of my peers kept spinning around in my head. We needed to act like a married couple, which meant while the press followed us around, we'd have to stay together. Whether it's at his house or mine, it didn't matter to the board. Just as long as we play the part.

"You're coming in with us, right?" I asked Candace, nodding toward the door when it opened, and our name was called. I at least wanted one person I knew with me while I tied the knot—or hangman's noose. Who knows which one it will end up being?

"Of course. I go where you want me to go." She smiled and stood with us.

I hugged her tightly, trying to keep my tears from staining her silk blouse. As I released her, I lifted my chin. It was time to put on my big girl panties and get married. "Let's get this over with."

Short and ... well, not so sweet. And not what I expected for my marriage. At the end we were asked if we wanted to share a kiss. I nearly choked, but Preston came to my aid. "She has a phobia of PDA."

Dumb excuse, but it worked for me. I didn't want my first kiss to be at my fake wedding.

When we arrived at the van in the parking garage, I was a mess. Per always, Candace knew what I needed and had packs of tissues on hand, and I needed them.

"Do you want me to drive?" Preston asked.

With a word, I handed him the keys and climbed into the back of the van, curled up in a ball, and cried. Yes, I no longer had my big girl panties on. Apparently, I needed to share diapers with Cas, because I was behaving like a pampered baby. But I'd always had a dream of a nice country wedding with my family in attendance. And I only ever planned to marry once.

This wasn't the track record I wanted for myself.

Twelve

Billie

What's the hardest part about football?
The ground.

We dropped Candace off at the office so she could take care of a few work-related things for me. We headed back toward my house, but Preston exited the freeway an exit too early. "Where are we going?"

Preston glanced at me in the rearview mirror. "Is it okay if I stop at my house? It would be nice to get a different set of clothing and start some laundry."

"Yeah. I guess you'd want to check on your home, too." We stayed silent until we reached his gated neighborhood. Preston paused before turning down a street.

"You'd better climb up front. It will look strange if you're not sitting beside me."

He was right, of course. Due to me wearing a skirt I didn't climb. I got out and slid into the passenger seat. Just like my own home, there was a gathering of reporters waiting at his house. Unfortunately, his house didn't have a large fence surrounding it to keep them from getting too close. Preston turned into the driveway as the crowd came crushing against the car to get a picture of the newlyweds.

He drove up the side of the house to the garage in the back. The reporters had the decency to stay on the sidewalk, but that didn't stop them from calling out questions. "Hang tight. Don't get out yet," Preston said then got out of the van. He jogged over to my door and opened it. He held his hand out to me with a smile.

I glared at him.

"For the cameras, my dear."

I rolled my eyes and took his hand. He eased me into his arms and kissed my head. My stupid heart betrayed me by jumping around like a goat with ADHD. He slipped his arm around me and we walked to the side door where he paused to enter a code. He swung the door open, bent, and lifted me into his arms.

I squeaked. "What are you doing?"

"Carryin' you over the threshold. Isn't that what I'm supposed to do?" He passed through the door, entering a large hall that led into a kitchen.

"For a real marriage maybe."

"But they don't know that it's a fake marriage." He nodded toward the door indicating the press in the yard.

"You can set me down now," I said and took in the rustic country kitchen we entered.

He lowered me but kept his arms around me.

I narrowed my eyes and pushed him away. "Don't press your luck, buddy. We're married in name only."

"You know, there was a night not long ago that I could have sworn you wanted to kiss me."

"Hum. I wonder what would have happened to have caused me to change my mind," I said in my snarkiest tone.

"Okay. I deserve that." He held up his hands. "But don't you wonder if this could work out between us?"

"No. Because it won't." I spun on my heel and walked into a living space that had no decor. The only thing that added character to the space was a beautiful stone fireplace with a rustic mantel, crafted from a halved tree trunk. Apart from that, the room was furnished with two recliner chairs, two end tables without lamps, and a single leather sofa.

"Not much happening in your house."

"I bought this house only a few months ago and I haven't hired a decorator yet. It needs a woman's touch, don't you think?" He grinned and swatted me on the butt. Being raised with brothers I wasn't shy to react. He didn't dodge my slug quick enough and grunted from the contact.

"Good golly, girl. You've got a mean fist." He chuckled and rubbed his chest.

"Let that be a lesson to ya." I lowered into the chair, pulled out my phone from my purse, and thought of all the insulting names I could call him.

He chuckled again. "I'm gonna go get my luggage from the car."

"Take your time." I tapped the icon to call Ivory. She picked up on the second ring.

"How did the meeting go?" Ivory asked in lieu of a hello. "Did they finally make a decision?"

"Yeah. And it's as bad as it can get."

"Oh, no. What did they say?"

I kicked my pumps off my feet and leaned back in the chair. "That there's nothing I can do to fix it other than get married."

"What? For real?"

"For real." Emotion crept into my voice again and tears began to fall.

"When is this gonna happen?"

"It already has." My vision blurred as I peered out the large windows into the backyard filled with trees, a pool, and a small gazebo.

"What?" Her voice turned shrill, and she started cursing. "I'm coming over. Are you home or at the office?"

I sniffed, realizing that I wanted to see Ivory, but also wanting to be left alone. "I'm at Preston's house."

"Why are you there?"

"There are reporters camped at both his place and mine. We have to appear to actually be together, so we're here for him to pack up a few things to stay at my house—in his own room, of course. We're not gonna go down that road because this is only gonna last for a few weeks or until people lose interest in us."

"Oh, honey. I'm sorry. How can I help?" I could hear the rustle of beads in the background and knew she was making some kind of jewelry.

"Well, we're supposed to show up in public every now and then and act like we like each other. Maybe you could babysit for me."

"I would love to. How long are you gonna be at his place? Do ya want me to come to your place later?"

"No. I'll be fine. I kinda want to just be left alone with some strawberries and my baby girl."

She laughed. "You and your strawberry fixations. How is Preston? Is he mad?"

"No. He's actually kind of annoyingly calm about it."

"Well, he is getting the better end of the deal."

"What do you mean?"

"You're a lot richer than him. And you're drop dead gorgeous. Of course, he is good lookin' too so it's not like you're gonna suffer."

My eyes grew heavy from all the crying I did. I closed my eyes and leaned back, pushing the recliner into a lying position. "He can't touch my money. He's signed papers."

"That's smart."

"Yeah." I started to cry again, sniffing into the phone.

"Talk to me, girl."

"I just wanted a pretty wedding dress and dancin', and all the good stuff. I wanted to have my daddy give me away to my new husband. I wanted a flower girl, and I wanted you as my maid of honor." I wiped the heavy tears from my eyes, careful not to smudge my makeup.

"I'm sorry, honey. I remember all those sleepovers and staying up late with you and Cas when y'all would gush about your wedding day. Y'all had such huge ideas."

"Yeah. And neither one of us got what we wanted." I sobbed some more then managed to squeak out, "I'm sorry. I'm just a big boob."

We both busted out laughing, remembering the response Preston had said a few days before. My tears still fell even though I laughed.

Once the giggling died down Ivory spoke again. "You said it yourself. You're not gonna be married to him very long. You'll still get your chance."

"You think someone would want me after all this junk?"

"Of course. The hardest part will be finding someone who doesn't know you're rich."

"Maybe I'll get a mail order groom." We both laughed at the ridiculousness of that statement.

I heard a chime on her end of the phone. "Someone's at my door. Can we chat later, honey?"

"Yeah. Talk to you soon."

After I hung up, I shifted into the chair, deciding it was quite comfortable, even if it was owned by a clueless slug.

Preston

Noah: **You're F-in kidding me.**

I rolled my eyes at Noah's response to my earlier text to the group. I lowered myself to the bed. I had to comment on his censorship.

Me: **What's with the F-in censoring?**

Noah: **I'm at my sister's house, and my niece can read and likes to steal my phone anytime I'm around.**

Koa: **Nice dude. Better keep UR phone locked or delete UR photos. Or better yet, DON'T LET HER GET YOUR PHONE, DUMBA**! And I guess we better watch what we text.**

Delany: **Can we get back to what Preston just said? UR married!!!**

Me: **Yeah. The vote was against us. But hey, it wasn't them getting married so what do they care?**

I stood from the bed, giving them time to respond. I had already unloaded my dirty clothes and started packing another suitcase full of clean clothes. From my closet I grabbed another suitcase to add more. My phone chimed again.

Noah: **Nice! So this is ur wedding night! Bow-chicka-wah-wow!**

His response did not surprise me one bit. I grabbed a few pairs of shoes from my closet and tucked them into the suitcase before I responded.

Me: **Married in name only and planning to only be married until the media forgets about us. Then we get an annulment.**

Noah: **No! Dude! I don't envy you. It's like standing in front of the only water left on earth and being told you can't drink it. She's too hot to not want to partake.**

Delany: **Noah. Think about it. They won't be married long and Billie isn't the kind of girl to have a fling. And I'm betting she wouldn't want that emotional attachment that came with it.**

Me: **Delany, how did you get so wise?**

Delany: **My mama slapped it into my head.**

I chuckled and texted back.

Me: **I need to run. I'm packing a few things to go stay at Billie's house and she's waiting on me.**

Noah: **Nooooooo! You're staying at her place and you don't get to hit that? F!**

Delany: You're screwed. Maybe you should just pull out the chick flicks and paint your toes or something.

Koa: Why R U staying there if U can't be with her?

Me: Reporters are at both our houses. Have to keep up appearances. Got to go.

I slipped my phone in my pocket, hearing it chime but not caring to see their responses until later. I rushed around my room throwing stuff I needed onto my bed. I went into the hall to go look for my extra charger for my laptop and stopped when I heard Billie's voice. By the sound of it, she was talking to someone on the phone.

"Yeah," she said, then started crying. "I just wanted a pretty wedding dress and dancin', and all the good stuff. I wanted to have my daddy give me away to my new husband. I wanted a flower girl and I wanted you as my maid of honor."

Guilt sucked the life out of me. I didn't hear the person's response, but I could tell someone was talking.

"Yeah," Billie continued, "and neither one of us got what we wanted." She cried harder, great sobs that tore my soul in half. Then a second later she whimpered, "I'm sorry. I'm just a big boob."

Billie's instant laughter warmed my ears. She was probably recalling my embarrassing vocal outburst from a few days ago that I wished I could forget. I cautiously backed into my room, trying not to make a sound. I shut my door and leaned against it. Regret grew, giving me a stomachache. I'd taken from her something she'd always dreamed of—well, maybe it's not all on me. But I had a bigger part to be blamed for. I just *had* to open my giant yapper and say something stupid to make the media's assumptions credible.

How could I ever make it up to her? I couldn't. Not unless we actually stayed married and threw a big party. Which was something I wasn't opposed to. Billie was the perfect woman. She's funny, smart, kind, strong, and independent. She's a fantastic mom and to top it all off, she's sexy as all get out, and I could stare into her eyes all day if she let me.

I couldn't say I was in love with her, but I liked her enough I wanted to find out if there was more. Which really hasn't happened in … well, never. At least not to this degree.

Hearing her cry pierced my heart. I hated hurting her. And I'd hurt her enough already.

My phone chimed and I checked the text from Koa that was not sent in the group text.

Koa: **Don't forget to get her a ring. The media has noticed her bare hand.**

He had sent a screenshot from an article that featured a photo of us with a red circle around her bare hand. I cussed and ran my hands through my hair. Then I remembered the ring my grandmother gave me—or left for me. It was her twenty-fifth anniversary ring. I kept it among my sock drawer, never thinking I would ever get it out. I dug through the drawer and found it in a ring box. I opened it to reveal the ring Mama had said was a vintage setting with one large diamond and several small ones running down the side. I had no idea it was vintage, nor did I know its worldly value. The sentimental value held strong in my heart, and I wondered for a moment if I should share this with Billie. The moment that question came into mind I knew the answer.

Yes.

She was just the kind of person to cherish something that meant something to someone. That much I could tell about her. I slipped it into my pocket and went about packing my stuff. I still hadn't unpacked everything from my recent move, so I had a few boxes lying around. If the press were watching the house and they saw me walk out to the van with a few boxes it would add credit to our marriage and show I was serious about moving in. I could even put my house on the market but not accept offers. I could drag it out as long as I needed then remove it from the market once the annulment went through.

This all could work.

I packed a few boxes with stuff I used on a daily basis when I was at home. I sent a text to my maid and asked her to do my laundry when she came tomorrow and asked her to take any perishable items from the fridge for her own use. Not that there was much since I was gone for a week.

I quietly exited my room, not wanting to walk in on a private conversation again. The only sound was soft breathing. I walked to the chair and smiled at her sleeping figure. *Oh, my lanta! She was beautiful!*

I squatted down beside the chair and watched her eyelids twitch. What was she dreaming? What thoughts occupy her mind on the daily?

I studied her cheeks and the curve of her jaw down to her neck and wondered if she would let me connect the dots of her freckles with my lips someday in the future. They covered most of her body. At least from what I'd seen. I reached out and touched her cheek with the tips of my fingers. Her lips twitched and made me smile. My fingers brushed down to her neck and moved back under her hairline.

She sighed and arched her back, which drove me crazy and had my blood pumping in my ears. Her lips twitched again, but her eyes remained closed. I slid my fingers to the curve of her neck and along her collar bone. She arched her back again and breathed heavily.

Dang. Delany was right. I was screwed.

I had to stop torturing myself and thinking I might have something more with Billie. I removed the ring from the box. I took her hand in mine and slipped the ring on her finger. I had no idea if it fit according to her desires, but it looked good on her slender fingers.

I brushed my fingers through her hair. "Billie. Hey, darlin." I kissed her hand. "Wake up."

Her eyes fluttered open. "Huh?" She blinked at me with brows pulled together. "Oh. Sorry. I didn't know I fell asleep."

"It's fine. I'm glad you could have a catnap." I squeezed her fingers so she might notice what I'd put there.

Her eyes drifted to the ring, then they widened. "Where did you get this?"

"It was my abuela's ring. It's vintage."

"It's beautiful." She stared at it a moment, blinking like she was trying to use her eyes for the first time. Then she removed it and held it out to me. "I can't take something that once belonged to your grandma. It's not right."

"Isn't that my decision?" I picked up a lock of red hair and twirled it in my fingers.

She pushed it toward me again. "I can't. Our marriage isn't really real. Not really. And I really can't accept something so valuable."

"Whether it's really real or not really real, I don't really care," I said with a smirk, then added, "Really. Wear it. My mom will notice and be happy about it. Besides, the media noticed you have no ring."

Her lips pressed together in thought. "I'll give it back," she whispered.

"I know." I tickled her jaw with her hair then poked it into her nose.

She half huffed and laughed, batting my hand away. "You're

such a toddler."

"I need to get you my jersey. I wanna see you where my name." *And nothing else.*

She shrugged like it wasn't that big of a deal. She'll learn soon.

"Shall we seal the deal with a kiss?" I asked.

Her eyes widened. She pushed herself up, kicking the recliner back into place before standing up. "You can't expect me to just kiss you. This is a marriage on paper only."

I stood and shoved my hands into my pockets. "And you don't think that people will expect us to kiss at some point?"

She lifted her chin, pressing her lips together. I could almost see the worry flickering in her brain.

"My mama is insisting we come visit her soon. Probably this coming weekend. I can guarantee she'll bully us into kissing for pics. Do you want our first kiss to be in front of people, or in private?"

She let out a heavy breath and closed her eyes. "Fine." She opened her eyes again. "But only *one* kiss."

"I won't push you, darlin'."

"Darlin'? Really?"

"Terms of endearment are always used in marriages. Get used to it." I stepped closer and rested my hands on her hips.

"You're enjoying this too much." She frowned and my grin. "Do you not see how disrupted our lives are gonna be from all of this?"

I shrugged, not wanting to let my usually destructive mouth kill the mood. Not that she was in the same mood I was in, but still. I couldn't allow myself to ruin whatever might happen. I lifted my right hand to rest at her neck, tickling my fingers into her hairline. Her body responded with a slight shiver. My other fingers caught at the hem of her shirt, and they touched bare skin. It was purely an accident, but from her response of closing her eyes and swaying toward me I gathered she liked it as much as I did.

I kneaded the back of her neck softly and moved my hand up the back of her shirt.

"What are you doing?" Her head lulled back. "I thought you were gonna kiss me," she asked.

I smiled. "I'm creating anticipation. A desire for the kiss. It's part of the fun."

Her eyes hadn't opened, and her chest rose and fell with her increased breathing. "Oh."

I removed my hand from her back and rested it at the other side of her neck, cradling her head in my hands. My thumbs brushed against her soft cheek. I leaned in closer so she might feel my breath upon her lips. They parted ever so slightly, and my knees weakened. I hadn't even started kissing her yet and she was driving me mad.

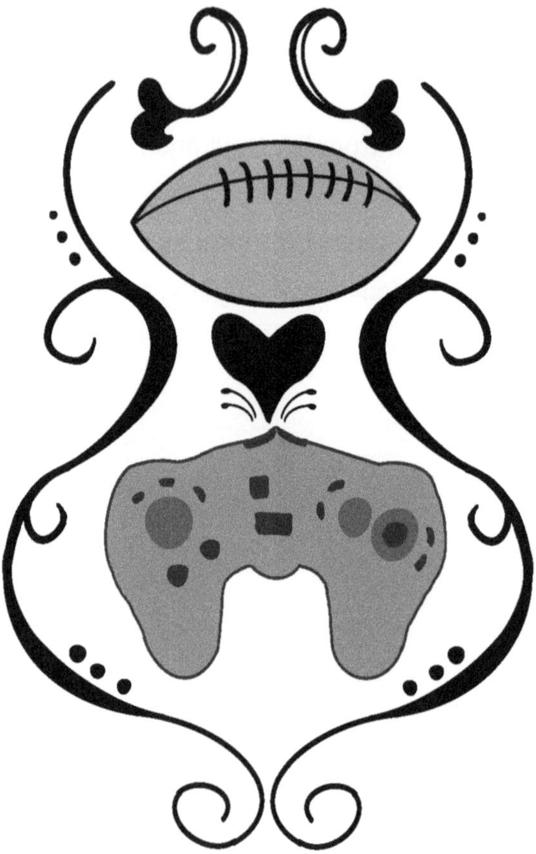

Thirteen

Billie

My wife said last night, "You treat our marriage like it's some sort of game"
Which unfortunately cost her 12 points and a bonus chance.

At last, they brushed, leaving a tingling sensation on my lips. Was he trying to torture me? To make a point that I wanted it? Yes, I admit. I wanted it. Who wouldn't? He was scorching hot and there was something smoldering between us. Of course I wanted his lips on mine. *Should* I, was the real dilemma. I hadn't been kissed, to tell the truth, so this was a big deal.

I had to get out of my head and not freak out over this. *Just relax and let it happen.*

His first kiss shot energy through to every cell deep in my bones. He eased away slightly then tilted his head, moving in again to press another tender kiss to my mouth. I moaned then sighed, reaching my hands up into his hair. He responded with more intensity, slipping his hands behind me and pressing me to him. Our lips worked together, moving as if in a perfect dance. He grabbed at my shirt at my lower back and deepened the kiss. A squeaking noise I had no idea I could create sounded from my throat.

His lips rose into a smile and a raspy chuckle bubbled from deep inside. He kissed me one more time, pulling my bottom lip between his. My knees gave way. Thankfully, he held me to him, or I would have dropped. I tilted my head back to take a breather. Something in his eyes made my breath hitch. I studied them. He studied me. What was he trying to say? Was it anything? Or was he trying to figure out what was happening too?

My phone rang.

I turned my head and cussed.

"That good, huh?" He chuckled.

"That's my mom's ring tone." I pulled myself—with great effort—from his arms and grabbed my phone from between the cushions of the chair. "Hi, Mama!" I answered, trying not to sound out of breath.

"I haven't heard from you," she said. "How did the meeting go? I've been worried."

"Sorry." My voice wavered. He slid his arms around me from the back, as if giving me support. "I'll be home soon to explain."

"Hurry. I need to run to the store and I don't want to have to wake Cas from her nap."

"I will. I'll be home within…" I looked at him in question.

"I'm done here. We can leave," Preston said.

"Is that Preston?" she asked.

"Yeah." I wiggled out of his embrace and faced him. "I'll explain in a few. Be home within fifteen minutes."

"Okay. Be safe."

"It's the only way to be," I answered as usual and hung up.

Preston smiled down at me and tugged me by the hips to move closer. I pressed a hand to his chest, hating that it was difficult to not want to caress it. "No. We can't kiss anymore unless it's necessary. That was our practice kiss. No more unless people are watching and expecting it."

He rolled his head back and groaned. "Fine."

I slapped his arm and stepped away from him. "You're such a baby."

"Yes. I am." He took me by the hand and led me into the hall. I followed him, my feet slapping against the stained concrete floors. We reached his room, but I stopped at the door and yanked my hand free. If he thinks I'm gonna get all lovey dovey just because we kissed once he had another thing coming.

He glanced at me, smiling as if amused. He pointed at the suitcase. "Do you mind taking that out to my car in the garage?"

Oh. He didn't pull me in here to make out and stuff. What a relief to not have to give him a black eye. That wouldn't go over well for our press conference tomorrow. "No. Not at all." I stepped into his room and lugged the suitcase out of the room and into the living room where I slipped my shoes back on. He had two cars in the garage, a Lexus SUV and a Jaguar. I didn't know which car he wanted to use, so I left it sitting between the two. I returned to find Preston juggling three boxes in his arms.

I hurried and took the box off the top. "What are you doin' with boxes? You're not really movin' in, ya know."

"I know that, but the press thinks I would be. So, I'm making it believable."

"You're really getting into this, aren't you?" I opened the side door since I had less in my hands.

"I don't do things half fast."

My nose wrinkled in confusion and helped him set things down. "Don't you mean half—"

He surprised me into silence by kissing my nose. "That too."

We loaded his SUV with his things then drove separately to my home. I drove home in silence, no music. I wasn't in the mood. I pulled into my garage, next to my Corvette.

He got out of his car that he parked in the drive and whistled when I exited. "You have a Corvette?"

"You didn't think I was only a minivan kinda mom, did you?"

He pointed at the other garage door. "What's in there?"

"Porsche Boxster and an F450."

We both walked to his car so I could help him unload. He kept glancing back at my car. "Why the F450? That's a pretty hefty truck."

"We have horses and need something to pull the trailer with."

His eyes got big. "You have horses?"

"Well, my dad does. I just keep them for him. He grew up on a ranch and since he started living here, he can afford to own horses again. So, I bought the truck and the trailer, he takes care of them and lets me ride them when I want. I call it a win-win situation."

"Where's your parents' car?"

"They park it in the side garage. They have an Audi R8, and they use my cars when they need to."

"I think I'm in love," he said as if dazed then pulled me in for a hug. "You have fantastic taste in cars."

I stiffened, glanced at the gate where reporters were filming then returned the hug, though reluctantly. "Can you stop now, please?"

He leaned away and smiled at me. "Sorry."

"Sure, ya are."

He handed me a suitcase to carry in through the garage. Once we had everything in the side door I shut the garage, cutting off any more opportunities for a media show. I let out a big sigh, feeling the tension ease, but the emotion of the day increased.

The second I saw my mama I burst into tears. Her eyes widened in concern. "What happened?"

Preston ran his hands through his hair. "I'll leave you alone with your family for a bit and unpack in my room."

Mama tugged me into a hug. "What did they say?"

"Mama. There'll be no weddin' dress for me." I stepped away from her and held up my hand to show her my ring. "I'm married. It's done."

Dad jumped up from the couch. "What!"

Preston

To say that a cloud of gloom hung over the evening would be an understatement. I didn't get the sense that the Leighs were upset to have me for a son-in-law. In fact, they seemed to like me. Maybe only because I played on their favorite football team. The gloom came from their daughter's dreams of choosing for herself the man she wanted to marry being flushed down the figurative toilet. And that she didn't get to have her dream wedding. Both of which I could understand. I too would have wanted a choice in who took my last name, bore my children, and stood by my side through my life. *Hold up... this might not get that far. Crud. This was getting confusing even in my head.*

But despite it all, I couldn't help but see a bright patch. Billie was the silver lining. Sure, dealing with her resentment and melancholy mood wasn't the best, but marriage wasn't ever all sunshine and rainbows for anyone. But Billie had so many more good qualities that I've learned about since meeting her in the hot tub.

My attraction to her was undeniable, skyrocketing from the moment I first laid eyes on her. Every time I got closer, that pull intensified tenfold. I could understand the concern and desire to keep our relationship out of the bedroom. Neither one of us wanted the possibility of that confusing mess if it didn't last beyond a month.

But as I sat with the family, eating our evening meal and

watching Billie play and talk with Cas, I couldn't help but wonder if there was any reason to fuss.

Looking back on my time on the ship, when I foolishly believed Josie's lies and pushed Billie away, I realized I couldn't go through that again. Just the thought of losing Billie made my entire soul ache.

"So, how long do you think this marriage will last?" Daisy asked, glancing between the two of us.

Billie locked eyes with mine for a moment as if asking the same question to me. She sighed heavily then answered, "As soon as the media forgets about us."

"How long do you figure that will take?" Nathan asked, pushing his empty place forward so he could rest his forearms on the table.

"Who knows," Billie answered without looking up. She'd hardly touched her food and I knew for a fact she didn't eat lunch. She only stopped pushing her meal around her plate when Cas would squawk in her highchair.

"We have a press conference tomorrow afternoon to announce ourselves officially and answer questions the press might have. Doing that will help get their many questions answered and possibly take us out of the direct spotlight."

"So, you're like, Mrs. Kyler now, huh?" Malcolm asked, taking his fourth serving of potatoes. Seeing him eat more made me feel better for my own fourth serving.

Billie's head snapped up then her face changed to full remorse. "Oh. I guess I am."

Seeing her reaction irked me. "Well, I didn't think my last name was all that terrible."

She glanced at me and lowered her head. "Sorry. It's not."

"What kind of questions do you think the press will ask?" Daisy asked, then stood to gather up some of the dirty dishes.

Billie peeked at me again as if I would answer.

"I hadn't thought of it," I answered and ate my last bite of roast.

"Well, you can be certain as the day is long that they'll ask how you met," Daisy said, placing the dish in the sink and rinsing it.

"I guess we'll have to come up with a story," I said, meeting Billie's gaze.

"I guess we'll need to talk this through to get our story straight." Billie stood to clear the table.

"Let me help." I gathered up my dishes and offered to load the dishwasher.

Daisy tugged on her son's arm and gave her husband a look. "We'll leave you two to talk things through. Have a good night. Holler if you need anything."

Billie gave her parents a hug then returned to the kitchen to help clean up. We both worked in silence, but I couldn't help the sense of unity I felt just by doing dishes together. It felt comfortable. Right.

By the time we were through, Cas's head bobbed around as she sat in her highchair. Each time her head lowered to a certain point she'd jerk back up with her eyes rolling. Billie softly giggled and pulled out her phone to take a video of it. I put my hand on her shoulder and chuckled with her.

"She's adorable," I whispered.

"She is."

"She's lucky to have you. You're a good mama, you know."

Billie didn't respond and she didn't have to. She slipped her phone into her yoga pants pocket and picked Cas up. "Come on, baby girl. Time to get you to bed." Billie held her close and kissed the top of her head. Cas mumbled and rubbed her dirty face into her mama's chest.

I couldn't quite explain why I followed Billie into Cas's room. Perhaps it was my fascination with the bedtime routine, or maybe

I just enjoyed watching the two of them together. For whatever reason, I leaned against the wall and watched.

"So, why do your parents live with you?" I asked.

"When I brought Cas home, I needed help getting used to caring for a baby. Mama came over every day so she was gone all the time and my dad didn't like that. It just made sense for them to save a little money and live with me for a while. I think they plan on buying a house nearby as soon as things settle down for me," she said and removed Cas's dress.

Did my mama blow on my belly like Billie currently did? The thought reminded me of my parents' request for us to come visit. "When would you like to go meet my family?"

"Where do they live?" she asked, tossing the diaper to the side.

"Corpus Christi."

She gave me a look like my comment was crazy. "I'm willing to go see your family, but we'll take my jet."

"I bet you're the envy of any parent travelin' with a child."

She didn't answer, instead she cooed at Cas and put a new diaper on her.

"How about we go see them over the weekend—not this weekend. My coach would kill me if I missed practice again so soon, but next weekend. Once the season starts though, my weekends will be filled."

"Right." She nodded once. "Sunday night football and all that jazz. I'll make the arrangements to fly to your parents. You have practice tomorrow?"

"Every weekday morning. Two of those days are practice with the team and the rest are individual training. But sometimes they mix it up. So, I have a lot of free time in the afternoons and evenings. Unless I have to do some kind of sponsor video or whatever they have me down for."

"Well, I'm pretty much at work until around four. Sometimes I get done earlier."

I smirked at her.

"What?"

"I bet you just sit around at work and play video games."

She gave me a deadpan look. "You think that's what I do all day?"

"Yeah."

"No. I do play at times, but most of my time is creating worlds, characters, plot lines—all the good stuff. I meet with all my teams and go over how I need them to program and design it. When there's an issue they need my opinion on, or if they want to show me something odd in the game, I'll play. The only time I get to play for fun is during a lunch break that I force myself to take, or at home with my brothers."

"That's rough," I teased. "Do you play the games from other competitors?"

"Of course. Where's the fun in gaming if you don't play it all? Plus, I like to see what might help me improve my games." She picked Cas up and rocked her from side to side.

"What's your favorite game outside of your own?"

"Zelda would be my first pick. Then Mario Kart."

"You and me, tonight." I pointed at her. "Mario Kart marathon."

She huffed. "You don't want to go there."

"Why not?"

She raised her brows and smirked. "I'd kick your trash."

I wrinkled my nose. "Ew. You like to kick people's trash? That's gross. What happens when you step on a banana or get a surprise diaper in the mix?"

"Ha. Ha. You're hilarious. But tonight won't work."

"Are you chickening out?" I grabbed my phone and pretended

to be looking at something while I took a picture of her snuggling her baby.

"No. I have a headache I need to control."

"I can help with that." I stepped closer to her to rub her neck.

She shied away from me. "I'm fine. It's nothing I can't handle on my own."

Once Cas was in bed, we settled down in the living room, she in a single chair, me on the couch. I leaned back, sprawled out my legs, and rested my hands behind my head. "I guess we should create a history."

"Yeah. I don't think it's going to work though."

"Why's that?"

She closed her eyes and rubbed her temples. "I'm terrible at lyin'. People will see right through it."

"Then we keep to the truth as much as we can."

"And what could we possibly say?" Her eyes were still closed as she rubbed her neck. "People think we went on a honeymoon cruise, so obviously we'd have to have gotten married before. But when? There's no option that makes sense."

"Is your head getting worse?"

She nodded and continued to talk. As she talked, I stood and walked to the back of her chair. "If we said we were married before it would have to be like the day or two before. Because—" she paused as my hands massaged at the back of her neck. "Be—because I've not mentioned you to anyone before the cruise, so my coworkers and friends will wonder about the marriage—um … you don't have to…" She moaned a bit, which got my heart rate going. "You don't have to do that."

I knew I shouldn't, but I also knew a massage was the best remedy for a headache. Having had plenty of massages to recover from tough games, I had a good idea of what to do. I pressed on, and her head lulled around in response. "How about we say that we met on the cruise, got married and upgraded to the honeymoon package. Or we met before and kept our relationship a secret from everyone. That happens, doesn't it?"

"I guess," she whispered.

"I think those are our only two options." I pressed my fingers along her neck and down the sides of her spine as far as her shirt would allow.

She leaned forward, breaking off my contact with her soft skin. It was probably a good thing due to where my mind was going. She adjusted her shirt forward. "Thanks. That helped."

Helped? I only massaged for like two minutes. I shook my head, feeling a bit dejected. "If you need more let me know."

She stood. "No. I'm good. Um. Let's go with the meeting on the cruise story."

"Are you sure? We might get backlash on that one. People will think I'm a gold digger, forcing you into a quick marriage to get your money."

She threw her hands up and let them drop. "I don't know. Then go with the secret relationship one."

She was visibly upset by how her chin quivered as if holding in her cry. "Hey." I stepped up and wrapped my arms around her. "It's gonna be okay. We'll get through this."

"We?" She stiffened and pushed away. "There won't be a *we* when this is over."

My heart found its way to my knees. She didn't want to even try? "Won't we still be friends at least?"

"Friends? What would have happened if Josie hadn't tried to stick her nose where it didn't belong, and you didn't get all weird on me?"

I flinched at the tone she used against me. "I would have kissed you and held your hand. And when we got home, I would have asked you on dates."

She narrowed her eyes, weighing my words as if she wanted to believe me but wasn't quite convinced. "And if you never found out I was a billionaire and didn't need your money?"

I rubbed my neck. "Well ... I would have been cautious."

"Because you thought *I* was the gold digger?"

It *was* the biggest concern I had moving forward with her. And I couldn't lie about it. So, I didn't say anything. Because I'm a chicken.

"You wouldn't have called me. You would have been too worried." She stood taller and squared her shoulders. "But I get it. I'm cautious too. There's a lot of freaks out there willing to go to extremes to marry me." She shot me a look.

I held up my hands in defense. "Woah! Do you think I did this on purpose to get your money? I didn't even know you were a billionaire until the very moment we were accused of being married and I was half drunk when I made that comment."

"Lower your voice. If you wake Cas, I'll hogtie ya and leave you for the buzzards. And I didn't think you did it on purpose. I'm just—" She rubbed her temples again. "I'm just frustrated and you're not exactly in my good graces right now."

"Why? Because I made a mistake and ran my mouth? I said I was sorry and at least I'm trying to make the best of it. We're gonna be together whether we like it or not, so the least you could do is be kind," I spat, grabbed my phone from the couch, and headed for my room.

Fourteen

Billie

Marriage is when a man and woman become as one. The trouble starts when they try to decide which one.

The bright lights flashed, making my headache pulse behind my eyes and tighten at the back of my neck. No matter what I did last night it still persisted. And the reporters calling out didn't help.

"Where did you two meet?" a woman called from the crowd standing around the large entrance of Legion Gaming.

My mama was right. First question even.

I discreetly nudged Preston and smiled up at him, batting my eyelashes. He smiled at me as his arm rested around my waist. "We met at a pool. I thought she was cute, so I asked her out. We dated secretly for a few months."

"I notice she has a ring now. Why did she not have one before? Did you want to keep the marriage a secret and if yes, why?" a man asked.

"I wanted to give her my grandmother's ring and it needed to be fitted." Preston pointed into the crowd. "Next question."

"You both seem to run things a little fast. Do you plan on giving your adopted baby siblings anytime soon?"

I laughed out loud then tried to reel it in. "No. One baby in diapers is enough for now, thanks."

Chuckles were heard all around.

"But you do plan on having more kids in the future?" a woman asked.

"Yes. I've always wanted to have lots of kids," Preston responded, and I tried not to react outwardly. His response kinda did funny things to my heart. Like it made his shortcomings a bit more tolerable just knowing he wanted to be a dad to many.

I man raised his hand but talked before he was chosen. "Can you tell us why you adopted your baby, Mrs. Kyler?"

My throat tightened, and tears threatened to spill. Why was this happening now? There were days I could think about Cassidy without shedding a single tear, so why was I getting emotional at this moment? I cleared my throat, trying to regain my composure. "My best friend died giving birth. She was like a sister to me and the least I could do was be a mom to her child." I turned to Preston. "I'm finished here."

"No more questions. Thank you."

"Can you give her a kiss for us?" someone yelled as more questions were shouted about our plans for our wealth.

Preston slid the other hand around my back. He leaned in and whispered. "Gotta put on a show." He dipped me, giving me a kiss to shoot me to the moon and back. I could hear cheers, but they sounded distant. All I could think of was warm lips and strong hands that supported me.

Perhaps I needed to thank whoever taught him how to kiss like this. Maybe give her a medal. Or at least a cake.

All too soon he raised me back up. Everyone chuckled. Probably because I looked dazed and stunned. He tucked me under his arm and walked me back to the elevator where Mike and Candace waited with a few people from the NFL crew. We chatted with them back in the conference room, going over the press release and how it would be received. Everyone seemed to be content.

Well, everyone but me.

Once we were through, I bid them good day and headed to my office for some needed alone time. I lowered myself into my gaming chair and spun around, facing away from the door. A knock sounded as the door opened.

"Hey," Preston said.

"Why knock if you're not gonna bother waiting for a response?"

He lowered himself to the floor next to me instead of taking the other gaming chair. "I just wanted to let you know that my PR rep *let slip*," he used air quotes, "to the press that we're gonna have dinner at the Mansion. He's made us reservations for seven."

"Why?" I asked, even though I knew why. "Don't answer. I know." I wanted to cry. But that was probably the reason for my headache. And I really should stop wallowing and buck up. "I'll miss seeing my baby."

"Maybe we can have your parents bring her. She can join us on our date, and we can send your parents on a date to have dinner, just the two of them. Do you think they'd like a date?"

I leaned my head back and stared at the icon for Legion Gaming that hung on my wall. "Okay. I'll text them and ask."

Preston pointed at the large TV screen. "Can I play?"

I nodded and started a game for him then went about texting Mama. She and Dad agreed to the idea and I asked for her to bring a change of clothes, even though I had a closet here to pick some clothes from. Going on a date for the media to see was like getting put in front of all the fashion critics of the world to nitpick to death what I wore. Thankfully, I had something fashionable to wear I'd purchased recently, so it wasn't out of date. Heaven forbid I wear my business suit I currently wore. If I had my choice, it would be yoga pants and an old punk rock band or anime shirt.

"Mama and Dad are gonna bring her." I rubbed my temples and gritted my teeth.

"Your headache hasn't gone away yet. Has it?"

"No. But I'm fine."

"Let me help you. I know how to stretch it and where to massage you to get headaches to go away."

I locked eyes with him. Honestly the idea sounded splendid. And at this point I would do anything for relief. But I didn't want him to become too comfortable with me, nor I with him. I debated back and forth for a few seconds before I responded. "Okay." I stood, removed my blazer, and sat sideways on the couch with my legs folded.

"Do you have lotion?" he asked.

I pointed at my desk. "Second drawer on the left." I adjusted my silk camisole so my cleavage wouldn't show too much and waited for him to settle down behind me. The second his fingers touched me, goosebumps spread across my body and every cell awakened. I don't know how he did it, but he could find each spot that was tight. His touch burned and I wondered if he was once a Boy Scout, because he knew how to build a fire.

How could I ever think I could pretend to be married to someone like Preston? Someone who brought me to life? Someone I'd lose control with?

Preston

My smile widened when Billie moaned softly. Did she know

she was even making any noises? All the quiet squeaks, sighs and moans were driving me nuts. Touching her freckled skin tortured me. Keeping my lips from connecting with her neck took all of my willpower. But I resisted because she needed help. Not a neanderthal draping all over her.

Just as I had the thought of it being difficult to massage with bra straps in the way she slipped them off her shoulders. I paused, trying to get my breathing back to normal. I moved my hands across her shoulder muscles and listened to her moan. "Right there. I think that's where my headache is coming from."

I gave the spot a good rub, pressing to get the knot out. Once I worked her shoulders I eased her toward me a bit. "Lay back. I'll massage you a bit more, then help you stretch your neck."

She did as I directed and laid back to rest her head in my lap.

Oh, crud. Now I could see more of her, and it didn't help one bit. I kept my eyes up so I didn't keep viewing her cleavage.

A knock sounded at the door, and I jumped. Jumped! As if guilty of being caught in bed with her.

"Come in," Billie called, but didn't move or even open her eyes.

Candace and one other employee entered. The other employee with the thick glasses spoke first. "I have the correction report for Scant 2 ready for your review."

"Wonderful. Thanks, Luke. You're flippin' awesome. Leave it on my desk and I'll look it over."

The man walked to the desk and dropped an envelope on the top of a stack of papers. He gave a quick goodbye and left with a smirk.

Feeling stupid and a bit guilty I pointed at Billie and spoke to Candace. "She has a headache I'm trying to help her get rid of."

Candace smiled. "Good. She needs pampering once in a while. She doesn't allow for that enough."

I smiled, grateful that she didn't think more of it. I continued to massage. Billie closed her eyes again.

"I wanted to go over your schedule for tomorrow," Candace stated and lifted a tablet in front of her.

"Go for it." Billie gave a thumbs up and listened to the meetings she needed to attend. She gave the approval and asked a few questions about other departments' progress and asked for chamomile tea to be brought in. Ten minutes later, a mug of tea rested on the end table as I continued to massage her in silence after helping her stretch her neck muscles. My hands ached from the effort, but I relished the excuse to keep touching her. Once her breathing steadied, and I knew she had fallen asleep, I gently lifted her head from my lap and carefully slid out onto the floor. She turned her head toward me and let out a great sigh. Her eyes fluttered under her lids as if dreaming.

Bravely, I leaned in and kissed her lips, as soft as I could, not wanting to wake her. She responded with a smallest of sighs. I smiled and sat back. Admiring her from head to toe. She was an extraordinary woman. Unlike anyone I've ever met. The conversation I'd had with her in the past about men doing anything they could just to gain her and her money came to the forefront of my thoughts. An urge to protect her grew.

If we split up and things turned sour—well, more than they were currently—who would protect her from all the creeps. She'd be hunted. And who's to say the man who caught her would treat her right?

Did *I* even deserve her?

I couldn't answer in the affirmative. No one would ever deserve her. I never could. I've done a poor job at even trying.

I covered her with a throw blanket then returned to playing the game I'd paused. Well, I physically returned to the game, but my mind wasn't in it. It still lingered at the couch and the beautiful woman that was slowly stealing my heart.

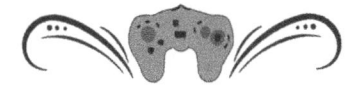

Billie

A breeze picked up, causing the candle at the table to flicker. Preston sat across the table from me on the outdoor patio. The trees with their twinkling lights slightly blocked the press's view of where we sat to dine. Preston held Cas in front of him while they played a growling game. Each time he would mimic her she would giggle.

I wanted to be mad at him. I wanted to keep him far away from my heart, but it was during moments like this that my heart betrayed me. Why does a man look even hotter holding a baby? It was doing crazy things to my ovaries.

The effect he had on me during the massage left me feeling disoriented, making it hard to function afterward. My headache did go away, like he had magic in his fingertips. My body warmed at the thought of his strong hands gliding against my skin. Just watching the muscles in his forearms now was making me lose my vertical hold.

Our food arrived, breaking me out of my wayward thoughts. Preston returned Cas to her highchair. She squawked and reached for the plate. Thankfully, it was out of reach. I moved a piece of carrot off to the side of my plate and cut it into tiny pieces for her to eat.

"What's your assessment of the press conference?" Preston asked, cutting into his lamb chops.

"It went well enough. I hope this will pacify everyone's curiosity then we can go back to being normal." I held a carrot out to Cas. She promptly took it and tossed it onto the floor. *Figures.*

"What's normal in your mind?"

I locked eyes with him, giving him a look to try to convey that now wasn't the time to talk of what would happen, not with all the press nearby. I changed the topic. "What would you be doin' right now if ... you know?"

He shrugged. "Probably doing something with Noah or Koa."

"Clubbin? Partyin'? What?" After taking a bite of my meal I gave another piece of food to Cas. She cried out and threw it on the ground.

He chuckled. "No. Possibly double dating. Noah was always pushing me into going on dates with him."

"How many of those women did you take out more than once?"

"None, really. Not the dates Noah found for me."

"So, you just do the one-night stand sort of thing?" *Why did that idea make me depressed?*

"No." He narrowed his eyes, holding my gaze with his. "Never that. Is that the kind of guy you think I am?"

"I honestly don't know."

He leaned forward and lowered his voice. "I'm not a virgin, like you are, but I'm not a player."

I stiffened and whispered, "How did you know I'm a virgin?"

He leaned back and glanced at the reporters, looking guilty. "Ivory told us."

My eyes widened. "Us?"

He lowered his voice even more. "Me and the guys. Back on the ship."

I sighed. "Great." *I'm gonna have a word or two with Ivory later.*

A stupid grin spread on his lips and I braced myself for what he'd say next. "You're cute when you blush."

Okay. That wasn't so bad. His foot still remained out of his mouth. For now, anyway. Cas started fussing and pulling on the headband I'd put on her.

He leaned forward further, almost getting his shirt soiled from his dinner. "Have you ever been tempted?"

My imagination has always been bursting with ideas, stories, and images. Creativity had always been present, so I'd imagined a lot of things. Being with someone had crossed my mind a time or two. Even the idea of being with him. But I couldn't say I was tempted enough to toss my values aside and become wilder than an acre of snakes. "No."

He took my hand and with his other hand ran his fingers across my knuckles and down my forearm. "Not even once?" My breath stuttered and my body weakened.

Cas screamed and arched her back. "Well, there goes the idea of eating all of my meal while it's hot." I laughed, nervously.

Preston stood and lifted Cas from the chair. "I've got her. You eat."

"But you need to eat too."

"We'll take turns. You first." He swayed from side to side with Cas grabbing his ear to inspect it. She'd calmed right down, just as she always did when someone held her. Not wanting to waste the opportunity, I ate the rest of my warm meal then took my turn caring for Cas while he ate.

Once we were finished and had Cas secured in the back of Preston's SUV, we started for home. Cas let us know the whole way back that she wasn't a happy camper. There was nothing we could do to soothe her. When I removed her from her seat after pulling to a stop in the driveway I felt moisture on my fingers. I checked her back and wrinkled my nose. "Ugh. She had a blowout."

Preston grabbed the diaper bag and my purse to carry inside. "A what?"

I held her up for him to see the dark moisture coming up from her diaper. "A blowout."

"Oh. Well. That's probably why she screamed the whole way

home." He chuckled. "What can I do to help?"

"Nothing." I carried her carefully into the house as she fussed the whole way. "I'm gonna go shower with her."

"Can I join?" he asked.

I gasped, gaping at him like he'd grown a new head.

He held up his hands and chuckled. "I'm only teasin' darlin'. I'll get a bottle ready for her." He kissed the side of my head before walking away.

Evidently, we needed to have a talk about boundaries.

Once Cas and I had showered, I wrapped her in a towel and myself in a thin robe. I carried her to the changing table and rubbed her down with baby lotion. The sweet scent wrapped around me, filling my heart with joy. Oh, I loved baby smells. As I zipped up her footie pajamas, Preston entered with a bottle and a smile. It wasn't lost on me as he looked me over that he liked what he saw. My whole head warmed.

I picked her up and lowered myself into the rocking chair, holding Cas to my chest. The instant I sat, my robe opened on my legs, revealing an entire leg. I tried to fix the problem, but Preston had already noticed. He held his arms out to me. "Go ahead and get dressed. I'll rock her to sleep and feed her the bottle."

I stood and handed her over. I kissed Cas's cheek then paused to look at Preston. "Thank you."

He moved Cas to one arm and with the other he touched my cheek. "You're welcome."

I stepped away. "Preston. You can't keep doin' that."

"Doin' what?"

"We're not a couple. There's no romancin' that's gonna happen between us. So, please keep your hands and your comments to yourself." I walked away before he had a chance to respond, because I was afraid of what he might say.

Fifteen

Billie

What's the difference between love and marriage? Love is blind and marriage is an eye-opener!

"Ride the horsey up and down. Turn the corner, don't fall down!" I bounced Cas on my knee, moving it side to side as if she turned the corner, then carefully leaned her back. She giggled and squealed in delight.

The second I stopped she began fussing. Flying in an airplane with a baby would never be on my top of the list, but it had to be done. It beat driving.

Preston returned from using the restroom and held his hands out to Cas. She leaned into him and snuggled into his chest when he took her. Over the last week and a half, she'd gotten used to him being around. He even had the ability to calm her and put her to sleep. I blamed his broad shoulders. Mine were too narrow and boney. His were firm, but soft enough to enjoy a nice lean. Not that I did. I made sure to keep my distance.

A minute later we were told to buckle up for descent. I peered out the window while Preston calmed Cas. The world below grew larger as we descended toward the small airport in Corpus Christi. Cas cried out in discomfort, so I pulled out the secret weapon and handed him the bottle. Soon we were taxiing to the building and slowed to a stop. On our way out I thanked my pilots and stewardess then climbed down the stairs. A bit farther off, a car I'd hired waited, along with a group of reporters, all clamoring to get videos and photos of us exiting the plane.

"Why do they still care?" I asked Preston who he pulled two suitcases behind me.

"I have no idea."

"How long do we have to keep this up?"

He frowned at me then mumbled, "I don't know."

Once we were in the car and buckled in, I brought the subject up again. "We've gone on a few public dates. And we've put up with them parked at our house. What more do they want?" Sure, the number of reporters had dwindled, but they were still there. Did they suspect the marriage to fail? I mean, it would. Eventually. But they weren't supposed to know that.

Preston remained silent except for the cooing and conversing he did with Cas. It hadn't taken him long to get down the whole baby-talk thing. He was a natural.

We soon arrived at a medium-sized home, possibly a three bedroom. As the car pulled into the driveway, two people rushed out of the house to greet us. When I stepped out, I looked between his mom and dad and realized he was the perfect blend of both.

Mrs. Kyler pulled me into an embrace, even though I carried a sleeping baby in a car seat. "Oh! I'm so happy to finally meet you!"

"It's good to meet you too, Mrs. Kyler."

"Oh, call me Carla. And call him Bob," she said and gestured to her husband.

I smiled and swung the car seat around. "This is Cas. My daughter."

Carla bounced on her toes and squealed with delight. "Oh! I'm a grandma now! *Ella es tan bella.* She's beautiful."

"Oh, I see how you are, Mama." Preston frowned. "Forget greeting your son now that you have someone better to pay attention to."

"Oh, you!" She grabbed Preston into a hug and kissed him. "You'll always be my favorite oldest son."

Preston peeked at me and shook his head. "You see what she's done there? What she really meant to say was I'm her favorite son. No *oldest* junk in there."

"Do I get to hug my beautiful daughter-in-law, too?" Bob asked and gave me a quick hug. I could see where Preston got his height and broad shoulders from. "Welcome to the family. You might regret marrying him once you get to know us."

I laughed, liking him already. Cas woke from all the chatter, cutting her nap short. She blinked up, confusion clouding her eyes. We entered the house with a living space, kitchen and stairs all visible from the entry. I removed Cas from her seat and held her on my hip. Carla showed us to a room down the hall where we would stay for the two nights we were visiting. When the door opened my body stiffened. In the corner under the window sat a desk, while on the opposite side of the room, against the sliding closet door, was a portable crib, neatly set up for use. The rest of the space was taken up by a queen-size mattress on the floor, made up and ready for sleeping. The only open area left was the three-foot square where we stood.

I looked at Preston and frowned. His eyes were glued to the bed.

"I know it's not what you're used to, but it's the only space we have," Carla said, appearing a bit nervous, most likely due to her small offering to someone who had means to have more. I didn't want her to feel like I was spoiled and would rather dismiss her kindness in having us stay.

"Oh! It's completely fine. I grew up sharing a room with my younger brother until we were older. I'm okay with it," I said, trying to make her feel at ease. Why I shared that fact, I don't know. Preston took my hand and squeezed, giving me a smile of gratitude.

"Well, dinner will be in a couple of hours. Grandma and Grandpa will be here to join us soon. And your sisters as well. Tomorrow we're having a big fiesta in the park. Everyone will be there."

"It will be good to see everyone," Preston said and stacked our suitcases to the side, taking away half the available space.

Carla held her hands out to Cas. "May I hold her?"

"If she'll go to you?" We tested it by moving her close.

Carla took her from my hip. "I'll go show her the fish while you get settled." She left with Cas staring at her as if trying to figure her out.

The moment she was gone I turned to Preston. "This isn't a good idea," I said and nodded toward the bed.

"What other choice do we have? Mama insisted we stay here." He removed his shoes and set them aside. "Might as well make the best of it."

"I'm afraid your idea of *the best of it* is far different than mine."

His brows rose. "Don't fool yourself, darlin'." He stepped close enough I could feel his breath in my cheek. His hands rested at my sides. "You're just as curious as I am."

My body shuttered. "Curious? No, I'm not."

He chuckled deep in his chest. "Right." His lips brushed against my neck, causing me to shiver again. I clamped my mouth shut to keep a sigh from escaping. He stepped back and grinned. "Not curious, my eye."

I glared at him. "You tickled my neck, is all. I shiver when tickled like that."

He gave me a look like he didn't believe me and left the room. He was right. Why did he have to be right?

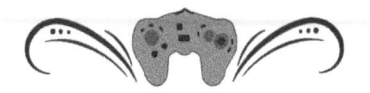

Billie

Carla's idea of a fiesta in the park was indeed a fiesta. She'd hired a band that played both Argentinian music and modern popular songs from the States. One of Preston's aunts had decorated with colorful flags, balloons, and streamers. A dance floor was set up next to the pavilion for those wanting to cut a rug. A large cake that said *Congrats Mr. and Mrs. Kyler* took up one end of the picnic table. The rest of the tables were filled with all kinds of potluck side dishes, meats, and desserts. About a hundred people showed up, all to celebrate mine and Preston's union.

A union that wasn't real.

The issue with all the lies was that I actually liked Preston's family. His sisters and I got along perfectly, like we'd always been friends. His brother was more reserved but was almost a copy of Preston in looks and build. He also played football and was in his second year playing for a university. Between Preston and Hector's teams their parents had a lot of games to attend once the season began.

They were awesome people.

Cas squawked to get my attention away from Preston and his

brother who tossed a football nearby. "Oh, I'm sorry. What were you saying?" I asked Cas, embarrassed that I'd been caught ogling Preston by an eleven-month-old.

Preston's sister, Gabriela, laughed and held her hands out to Cas. "Can I hold you, sweetpea?"

Cas grinned and let herself be taken. A four-year-old cousin, Anna, I believe, hung about due to a baby being present. She crowded in to coo at Cas. Anna wrinkled her nose and waved her finger at Cas when she tried to take a fist full of Anna's dark curls.

"She likes my hair." Anna giggled and leaned away. She grinned up at me then wiped her nose with her arm, leaving a trail of snot across her cheek. I fought to keep from gagging and laughing. Her eyes lit up before asking, "Does she like special drinks?"

"She likes milk mostly," I answered.

"I make her a milkshake." Anna bounced off toward the end of the picnic table where the large cooler of Kool-Aid sat. I don't know where she'd get ingredients for a milkshake, but at least she had a goal, ambition, and probably an imagination.

Carla, who had paused her conversation with her sister, put her empty plate aside and turned to me. "Billie, do you know how to dance?"

"I do. My mama was an instructor."

"So, you must be good," Preston's aunt—I'd forgotten her name already—asked.

"Preston and I won a dance competition when we were on our cruise, so I think I'm half decent."

"Oh! I'd love to see you dance!" Carla said then whistled and waved at Preston.

He glanced over then tossed the ball to Hector before jogging back to the pavilion. "Yeah, Mama?"

"I want to see you two dance." Carla pulled me to my feet then waved at the dance floor. Before anything more could be said Anna returned with a cup full of liquid and a big snotty grin.

Anna held the cup up. Bits of grass and other unidentifiable floaties swayed with the motion of the pink and brown liquid. "I made Cas a drink."

"Oh! How sweet of you!" No way was I letting my baby drink whatever was added to that cup. "But I'm sorry, honey. She can't drink out of those kinds of cups. Only bottles."

Her smile fell. "Oh." Then as quickly as her smile left, it returned again when she shifted the cup in Preston's direction. "I made you a shake, Presson."

He chuckled and raised an eyebrow in my direction. "A milkshake, huh?"

"Yep." Anna held it out to him.

His giant hands wrapped around it. He peered in. His Adam's apple bobbed. "It looks ... great."

"I drank some to make sure it tastes good, and you don't die," she said then her little pink tongue slipped out and drug through the snot resting on her upper lip.

A whimper came from Preston's tightly shut mouth. Everyone around watched with dancing eyes and huge grins.

"Go on, Preston. Guzzle it down," I said with laughter I tried to suppress.

"Yeah, it's delicious!" Gabriella added.

Preston gave a nervous chuckle again then lifted the cup to his lips. I held back a gag and tried not to think too much about the ingredients of the milkshake ... or the snot. He lifted the cup, only letting the liquid touch his upper lip, never opening his mouth. He lowered it, rubbed his belly, and grinned. "Mmmm. You are a master chef, Anna."

"Cheater," I whispered through the side of my mouth.

"Shhh," he responded in the same way.

Her dark curls bounced from her swinging leg that picked up speed at his compliment. "I'll make you more!"

Before she could turn to leave Carla stopped her. "He's gonna dance with his wife for a bit, so you better wait until next time, Anna."

"Okay!" Her eyes got big, and she gushed out, "Will he dance with me too?"

"You bet, kiddo. But my wife gets first dance." Preston slipped his hand in mine. Butterflies took flight in my stomach.

Carla instructed the band to play a Latin song while Preston took my hand and placed his other at my back. I narrowed my eyes. "Remember that we're dancing in front of your family, so let's not get too steamy like on the cruise."

A smirk grew, drawing my attention to his perfect lips. The memory of our first kiss invaded my thoughts, but I quickly shoved it out like an unwanted guest. "That was pretty steamy, wasn't it." He wiggled his eyebrows.

I rolled my eyes but couldn't help the slight smile that tugged my lips. Preston guided me into step with him, dancing salsa to the tune. He did a good job and kept us in motion away from each other. The family gathered around, cheering us on and joining in the fun.

When we finished, he held me closer and lowered his lips to mine, in what I first thought would be a quick kiss like he'd given me over the last day when his family was watching and had been expecting stolen kisses. This kiss wasn't quick. He went in for another, then another. Each time I responded accordingly and felt the tingling to my toes. But then *I* took it too far. I don't know what I was thinking, but I gently tugged his bottom lip with teeth.

A husky growl rumbled up from his chest and he responded with eagerness, holding me closer. When the family cheered and cat called, I pushed back, feeling heat in my cheeks.

His eyes searched mine, and his small smile made me wonder what was going on in his head. Honestly, I was unsure about my own feelings. Did I really want this? Could I trust him not to throw me away again if I opened my heart to him?

He pulled me in for another short kiss then guided me into another dance. What would happen if I let him in and he destroys me? How much worse would it be now that our families were involved?

Maybe I didn't want to know the answers to those questions.

Preston

In the silent, dark room I tossed my shirt on top of my suitcase, careful not to make any noise so I wouldn't wake Cas who had gone to bed three hours before. It was late and Billie would skin me alive if I woke Cas. I laid down on the mattress and fluffed my pillow. The door opened and Billie's form in her silk shorts and top was lit up by the dim light of the hall. I groaned inwardly. Silk and soft skin. Torture.

No. It's fine. We slept by each other last night without much issue. Sure, I had to think of things other than her next to me, but we did it. I could do it again.

My phone chimed and I checked the message, thankful I had something to occupy my mind as she climbed over me to reach her side. The new message had me cringing.

Hi sexy! This is Cassidee. I borrowed a phone to text

you. I'm thinking of you, baby. 🖊 I miss U, honey!!! I know we've had our differences, but I think we were meant to be. I love U. Please call me.

Along with the text she sent a picture of her looking seductively at the camera with a camisole top barely hanging on her shoulders.

I wanted to chuck my phone across the room and never see Cassidee's texts again. Each time her texts would come in on a different number so I couldn't keep her from contacting me. She texted last night as well. And three days before that. Each of my responses were the same:

I'm married. Leave me alone.

How thick headed could she be?

I slid my phone back to the side of the mattress after turning it off.

"Who was that?" Billie asked.

"No one. Just annoying texts."

"Noah then?" I heard the humor in her voice and turned to see her lying on her side, gazing at me. My heart skipped a beat.

"Yeah," I answered, not connecting my brain with my mouth.

Another chime sounded, but didn't belong to my phone. "Oops. I should check that then turn it off." She leaned over me to reach her phone. Her long hair hung and tickled my face. My heart and imagination went wild. From the light of her phone's screen, I saw her brows furrowed as she read her text.

"Is something wrong?" I asked, my voice sounding funny and deep to my ears.

"Mama and Dad are gonna go visit with my aunt tomorrow.

They'll be gone for a few days. I guess my aunt's having marital problems and needs support. I'll have to call a neighbor to have them care for the horses." A second later her phone turned off.

When she placed her phone down, her chest pressed against mine. It undid me. I reached up and pushed my fingers through her hair behind her neck and eased her in. She didn't put up a fight. Instead, she lowered to me and our lips met.

She moaned and her leg moved over mine. I held her to me as we kissed, caressing her anywhere she'd allow. Her hands drug through my hair and down one side of my bare chest. I'd been dreaming of the moment we'd be holding each other this way and it felt far more incredible than I thought possible.

She pushed away, dropping to the side to get off of me. I followed her, keeping our lips locked. Her breathing was quick and shaky, matching mine. My lips explored her jaw then down her neck, enjoying her softness and the smell of sweet perfume. Her back arched when I grabbed at her hip. She moaned my name.

I shifted to her ear and nibbled with my lips on her lobe. "Yes, darlin'?"

"We have to stop."

My hand went from her hip to her ribs. "Why?"

She pushed against my chest, and I eased away, but keeping my hand on her waist. She struggled to catch her breath. "For starters, Cas is in this room."

"Oh, yeah." I couldn't believe I'd forgotten that.

"And for another, I'm not going down *that* road in your parent's house."

Did that mean she'd want to travel down that road if we were somewhere else? I might have to test that out later. "Then what if we just make out?" I nuzzled my lips into her neck.

"Oh," she said, breathlessly. "Okay." She ran her hands into

Christine M. Walter

my hair and tugged me to her lips. I gladly obeyed.

Sixteen

Billie

I asked seven billionaires, "What's the secret to your success?" They all said the same thing! "How did you get into my mansion?"

Preston's lips on my shoulder woke me the next morning. Those same lips moved down my arm then up again, trailing along my neck. I sighed and turned to face him. I smiled and brushed his hair back from his face. "Hi."

"Good morning, beautiful Billie."

My heart soared at his words. Knowing that he saw me as beautiful warmed my heart. He leaned down and pressed a gentle kiss to my lips, seemingly unbothered by any morning breath. I willingly kissed him back.

He kissed along my cheek then under my ear. "I could get used to waking up next to you."

So could I, but something held me back from saying it. What was he implying with his declaration? Did he like me enough to call it love? Because I think I might be feeling something more. I giggled when Preston nuzzled my neck again.

Cas's head lifted and her dazed eyes searched the room. *Rats.*

"Oh, I woke Cassidy."

"I've got her," Preston said, getting up to lift her out of the crib. He set her on the bed with me to snuggle, then resumed his place beside me with Cas between us.

Cas's sleepiness faded into her typical morning comedian in a matter of minutes. We all giggled and she rolled around us on the bed. The whole experience warmed my heart even more, watching Preston play with Cas. It was in that blip of time that I understood what I've been feeling over the last couple of days. Love for him grew in my heart. My heart had opened to him and I wasn't quite sure what to do with that or if I should share that information with him yet.

What if he didn't love me?

A knock sounded on our door. "Come in." Preston called then laughed when Cas poked him in the nipple, acting curious as to what it was.

Carla opened with a smile and took a picture of us. I covered my face but did it too late. "Oh, my good gravy. I look terrible."

"Y'all look adorable," Carla said then tapped at her phone. My attention went back to Cas who, at the moment, had a red face and was making grunting noises.

I laughed. "Looks like we'll need to change a diaper here pretty quick."

Preston wrinkled his nose and then plugged it. "Jeesh, Cas. Why do you have to be such a baby?" He picked her up and handed her over to his mama. "Here. Take her away."

I slapped his arm and laughed. "Rude."

Carla gladly took her. "I'll change her and get her fed. You two get ready for the day."

The door shut and Preston attacked, grabbing me around my waist and kissing my neck. I shrieked and giggled, loving his playful

Games of a Billionaire

side. We made out for as long as we thought we could get away with before we went about getting ready.

After lunch I received a text informing me the hired car had arrived and waited outside to take us back to the airport. Preston took the luggage out and I carried Cas in her car seat. We said goodbye to Preston's family with promises of returning soon, then drove back to my awaiting jet.

Once in the air and able to walk around the plane, I headed into the bathroom for a break. While I washed my hands, I thought about what I wanted from our relationship. When I looked at all the qualities that made up Preston Kyler, I realized he really was the right guy for me. We might have had our struggles, but he really was a good man. A kind man. By the time I finished I had the determination to tell him I wanted to move the relationship to the next step.

When I got closer to where he sat, facing away from me, I overheard something that had me pausing, listening to his phone conversation. "No. She's not gonna understand that there can't be a relationship between us." He paused. I stood rooted to the spot, wondering what he meant. "Because it's Cassidy. She's gonna ruin everything and my career will suffer."

Cas? What has he got against Cas?

My heart dropped and made residence in my feet. With each step I took to return to my seat it felt as if the words he'd said had crushed my heart to bits. I paused and instead of taking the seat beside him I sat across from him and glared out of the window.

When Preston saw me, he quickly ended the call. "Hi, gorgeous. Everything okay?"

I gave him my best smile under the circumstances, but I felt it go flat. "Fine." I wasn't fine. I'd just had my heart slapped around and I also had a scratchy throat and a headache coming on.

He studied me with narrowed eyes. "You sure?"

Act normal. Don't let him suspect anything. You can't fall apart now. I gave him a better smile and nodded. "I just can't wait to get home."

"Any reason you didn't sit by me? I've been liking our closeness."

"I'm kinda getting a scratchy throat, so I'll just keep my distance for a bit." I sat back and closed my eyes, grateful Cas had gone to sleep for the ride home.

As we got closer to home, I could feel my earlier claim about having a scratchy throat becoming more accurate. My body weakened with each passing minute, chills started to creep in, and a pounding headache throbbed against my skull. All I wanted was to collapse into bed.

But I couldn't. Preston had made his thoughts known about his feelings toward Cas. He saw her as a burden. He didn't think we could have a relationship because of her. Since that was the case, I dared not let him get any closer to her, nor did I want his help with her. She was my baby, and I alone would take care of her. I was the one that wanted her, not him.

When we arrived and endured only a few of the reporters outside our gate—why they'd wait around for days in their cars, I never could understand—we pulled to a stop at the front door. With shaking arms, I lifted Cas and her car seat out of the back.

"Darlin'. You look like you're gonna pass out. Let me get her for you." He reached to take her, but I swung her away.

"No! I'll take care of my own." I nearly stumbled over trying to step away from him.

"Billie?" His eyes narrowed, watching me with confusion. I hurried away from him before he could try to help again. I made it into my bedroom seconds before I dropped to the floor beside my bed, panting. Cas had woken and was fussing with a red face.

"I've got ya, baby girl." I removed her from her chair with strength I didn't know I had. When I touched her skin, my worry increased. She was hotter than blue blazes. I'd never dealt with a sick baby before and instantly worried about what I should do. I grabbed my phone out of my purse and dialed Mama.

"Hi, honey. Are ya home?" she asked.

I'd stupidly left the door open, so Preston took it upon himself to enter and lower to the floor next to me.

"Yeah. Mama, I'm sick and I think Cas is sick too. What should I do?" I asked and Cas whimpered into my chest.

Preston's penetrating gaze switched to concern. He reached for Cas, but I moved her away.

"For starters, there's a thermometer in the bathroom closet. Keep track of her temperature and if it's high I would recommend sittin' in front of a fan with only her diaper on. That always worked for you kids."

"Is Malcolm home?"

"He moved into his dorm this weekend, remember?"

No! Who's gonna help me? I can't do this while sick too. "Oh, yeah. When will you be home?"

"Not for three days."

Mama gave me a few more instructions on how to care for her then said goodbye with demands of me calling her later to check in.

"You're both sick then?" Preston asked.

"Yes." I growled then stood, holding Cas to me. My body protested with every step out of my room.

"Billie, what can I do to help?" He followed, trying to take Cas from me.

I twisted so he couldn't reach. "Nothin'."

"Billie, you're obviously not feeling well. Let me help."

"I can do this myself." I stepped into the bathroom and opened cupboards to search for the thermometer.

"Do you realize how foolish you're sounding, Billie? I'm here with nothing to do. Let me help you." He opened a door and grabbed a container to search.

I turned on him, shooting flames at him through my eyes. "How dare you stand there and act like ya care. All ya care about is your career."

He jerked his head back as if slapped. "What? I care. I care about you a lot."

I huffed. Yeah. He cared about getting me in bed, but not about a relationship with me or my daughter.

"What's gotten into you, Billie?"

"Will you please leave?" I found the thermometer and pushed past him, Cas crying and rubbing her face into my neck all the while.

"Honey, I'm not gonna leave when I can help. Let me take Cas and you go lie down. I'll warm you up some soup and—"

"No!" I yelled, making Cas jump and cry harder and making my throat hurt more. "I want you to leave my house. Go home. You're not wanted here anymore."

He stepped back, looking like I slapped him with a dead possum. His eyes turned hard. "Fine. If that's what you want." The door slamming after him reverberated through the house, breaking my resolve.

Preston

I had bought my home just three months ago during the start of the Arizona heat, drawn in by its inviting floor plan, imagining it as the perfect place to raise a family once I found the right woman. But now, it sat cold and lifeless, and that woman seemed out of reach.

She had slipped away like smoke, vanishing from my grasp.

Just when I thought Billie and I were making progress, she pulled out a figurative shotgun and shattered everything into pieces. I had even started to admit to myself that I was falling in love with her. I did love her. Still do, if I was being honest. But now I'd wished I'd kept my distance and not tried to push a physical reaction from Billie. I knew she was attracted to me. I could sense it and I tried to help her open that up and see it too, but now I realize I'd made a mistake. I should have left well enough alone.

The alarm went off, reminding me to get my butt out of bed. Two days ago she'd kicked me out, but I couldn't wallow every day. I had practice that I couldn't be late for. Pushing my loneliness and thoughts of Billie out of my brain, I went through my morning routine to get myself out to the car. As I backed out of the driveway my unease increased.

There were more reporters, not less. Why were there more reporters?

When I reached the stadium for practice, I noticed another group of reporters waiting, this time I didn't have a car to protect me or fellow team members to walk in with me.

"Mr. Kyler, can you tell us what happened between you and your wife?"

"Have you two separated, Mr. Kyler?"

Oh, no. They know.

How do I fix this?

"Was your marriage a fake to begin with?"

"There have been reports that you faked the marriage. Is that claim true?"

"What? No!" I said, feeling fed up with these people. "Look, she's just sick and didn't want to get me sick so she sent me home."

"So, you left your sick wife to fend for herself?"

"She has family, and she didn't want my game to suffer by being sick." I pushed through them. "Excuse me. I don't want to be late."

I channeled all my pent-up irritation toward Billie and all the reporters into practice. So much so that the coach laid into me for getting reckless. He didn't want me injured before the season even started. Neither did I. I needed to make things right. To some degree, at least. Whether Billie liked it or not I had to go back to her place to stay.

When practice was over and I'd showered and dressed, I checked my phone. No messages from Billie. There was a message from an unknown number, so I dialed into voicemail to listen.

"Hi, honey." a familiar sultry voice said over the line. *Josie. Great.* "It's been so long since I've gotten to spend time with you. I've been busy, but I was hoping we could get together. I can't stop thinking about the kiss we shared. Maybe I can come visit and watch you practice. Then we can finish what we started."

I groaned and put my phone in my pocket. A hand came down on my shoulder. Koa grinned. "I heard the coach reamed you one for getting a little overboard. Trouble with the missus?"

I flung the door to the locker room open and walked out with Koa at my side. "She's sick."

"And you're worried?"

I shrugged. I was worried, but I wasn't about to call her to find out how she was fairing. She'd probably flog me for caring.

"What happened?" Koa asked.

I knew I couldn't hide anything from Koa, so I confessed. I briefly told him about how we kissed. A lot. Then how strange she acted on the way home and how panicked she acted about Cas being sick. Koa nudged my shoulder. "You know what I think? I think she's worried and acted out. Think about it. When people are scared, they act irrationally, maybe she just needs someone to take her fear away."

"Like how?" I asked and opened the outer door. Beyond the fence, the reporter waited so we stopped to finish our conversation.

"Go back. Don't let her push you away. Show her you'll take care of her. Fix her dinner. Stuff like that."

Wow. Maybe he was on to something.

Maybe if I just show her some tenderness and take care of her and her sweet Cas, then she'll see things differently. Maybe she didn't hate me and she was only tired and scared. I slapped Koa on the shoulder and thanked him. He walked with me through the crowd of reporters, helping to block them when needed. Once in the car I went through my game plan for helping Billie to feel better. To feel less stress of being a mother, and to feel safe with me.

Along the way I received a phone call from my disturbed PR adviser. The news was spreading about our "break up." He insisted I fix the problem. I told him I would and that I had a plan.

A couple of hours later I arrived back at Billie's house with my luggage and bags of groceries. I carried my load in, taking more than one trip. Each time I hurried between the house and the door, reporters shouted questions at me from down the drive. I ignored them and piled everything just inside the side door next to the laundry room.

With a few bags in hand, I entered the main part of the house, pausing in shock at the sight before me. Dirty rags and soaking towels were strewn across the floor in the kitchen, like something had been spilled but only cleaned up part way. Dirty baby bottles and other dishes filled the sink. A pile of dirty diapers in the hall gave the house its unpleasant aroma. When I walked in further, I found Billie on the couch, hair up in a messy bun and wearing only a towel that nearly had come undone. Cas lay in her arms, bottle hanging from her teeth. Both were asleep.

I carefully set the bags down on the counter before making my way to the couch. As I got closer, I noticed the goosebumps on Billie's inviting legs and arms. I grabbed a nearby throw blanket and draped it over her. Neither one of them stirred, so I went about putting food away. Once I finished that, I cleaned up the spilled mess on the floor and tossed the towels in the laundry. The floor was still sticky, but I decided to worry about that once dinner was through. I started making a chicken soup recipe that my mama had texted to me by shredding a rotisserie chicken. The downfall of my idea of making a meal came when I had to retrieve the large pot out of the cupboard.

The noise woke Cas, who started to whimper. I hurried to her side and picked her up from her mother's arms. The movement woke Billie, who jerked awake and screamed. Which caused Cas to cry harder.

"It's okay, darlin'. I'm just here to help," I said to Billie, then kissed Cas, bouncing her in my arms to calm her.

Billie started to sit up then pressed her blanket to her chest. "I'm not dressed! You shouldn't be here!" Her outburst made her cough.

"Calm down. You're scaring Cas. And it's not like I'm gonna do anything to you." I carried Cas into the kitchen with me and watched Billie sit up from the corner of my eye. She wrapped the blanket around her and rushed toward the hall. Her towel fell from under the blanket, causing her to bounce unsteadily against the corners of the walls.

"Are you okay?" I asked, now watching her fully.

She didn't fall and righted herself in the end. "I'm fine!" she snapped and disappeared down the hall.

Cas had calmed down and leaned into me. I placed the pot on the stove and snuggled her. "Your mama is a hard one to figure out, Cas. You're not gonna be that difficult, are ya?" She lifted her head, watching my face. "Nah. You and I are gonna get along fine." I laughed and kissed her cheek. "Any pointers you might have to win your mama over?"

She babbled and shoved her fingers in her mouth.

"Huh. I'll have to think about that one." I dumped the onions and celery I'd chopped into the pot with butter, all one-handed. Thankfully, I'd chopped everything before getting the pot out. "One thing's for sure: her looks are gonna drive me crazy." I tickled Cas's belly. "Do you know your mama is a hotty? She is. Of course, you and I probably shouldn't be having this conversation, but dang! She's got nice legs."

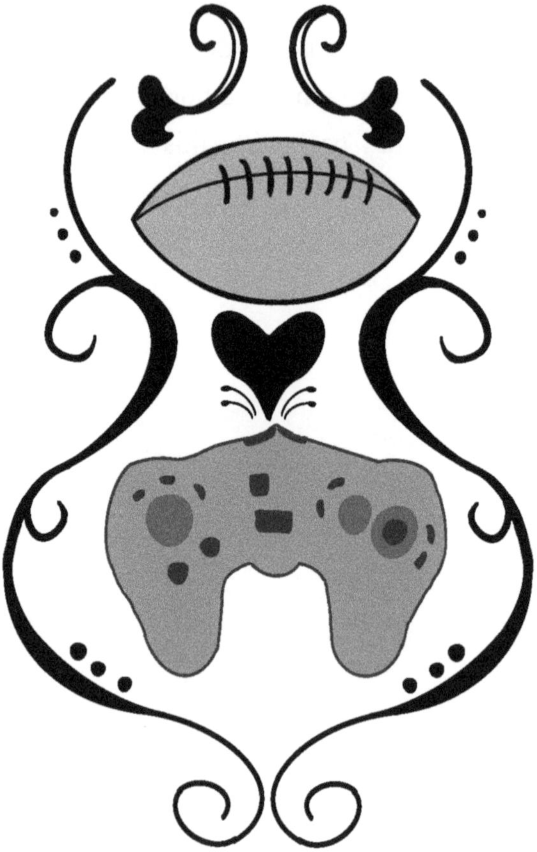

Seventeen

Billie

What happens to football players who go blind? They become referees.

I narrowed my eyes. What kind of crap is he discussing with my daughter? Though part of me was flattered he thought I had nice legs, a bigger part of me wanted to sock him in the nose. "Can I have my daughter back now?"

Preston jumped, then spun around, his shoulders rising up to his ears. Guilt at getting caught oozed from him. His eyes traveled over my appearance. I didn't care if I wore lounge pants, had a baggy sweater on, and my hair was a mess and stuck to my face from having sweat to death earlier. I wasn't out to impress him. I leaned heavily on the counter, trying to stay upright and not shake too much.

"You look as though your hopper's busted." He had the gall to smile at me. "Need a hand getting back to the couch?"

"I'm fine," I said through gritted teeth. Another tickle in my throat built up too much so I coughed once again. Had I the strength, I would already have my baby away from him and be in the process of tossing him out. "What are you doin' here?"

"Fixin' dinner. You look like you're gonna fall over if someone sneezes. Go lie down, darlin'. I'll take care of Cas and dinner. You rest." He placed his hand at the small of my back to guide me.

I shoved his arm away and walked on my own. I dropped into the couch. "Leave Cas with me. We wouldn't want her to be a burden on you, now would we?" I glared at him.

His brows pulled together. "Why would she be a burden?"

I didn't answer and he seemed resolved to accept my lack of explanation. He kissed Cas on the cheek, which made me wanna slug him, then lowered her next to me.

"Do you like chicken soup?"

"Why are you doin' this? Why are you back? I told you to leave."

"We have an issue we need to resolve." He lowered to sit on the coffee table, making us eye level with each other. "It seems like the press got wind of me being kicked out. So, we need to repair that image being painted of us. They seem to think we faked the marriage."

"We did," I spat.

His sad eyes studied me. "What happened? I thought we were doin' fine. Why did you kick me out?"

"Like you care. All you care about is your career and saving face through this." *Great. I sounded like a spoiled teenager.*

"That's not true." He peeked into the kitchen. "My onions need tending. We're not done talking about this. And get used to me being here. The moment I leave it will confirm what the media is saying."

He stood and hurried back into the kitchen. Cas wanted to play on the floor, so I let her down and watched her crawl around. She found her toys in the baskets, then crawled back to me, pulling herself up to stand with her face next to mine to show me what she'd brought. She would then remove her pacifier to babble at me. Seeing her moving about like a normal baby once again eased my mama heart. It was the first time in the last two days that she did anything other than sleep and whimper. I still felt weak and hungry—really because I focused on feeding Cas and only ate string cheese and strawberries—but my headaches, body aches, and fevers had passed. In truth, chicken soup sounded like heaven.

A few minutes later Preston returned to the couch and sat down on the floor next to where Cas played. "Girl, no offense, but you smell ripe."

"She needs a diaper change," I started to cough and sat up to my elbow but stopped when Preston jumped back up.

"No. Stay there. I'll go get the stuff and you can teach me how to change her." He hurried away, leaving me confused. Why would he say one thing, then do the exact opposite? He said Cas would ruin his life. He couldn't like her if he thought that, so why would he act as though he loved her and adored her?

He returned with diapers and wipes in hand. When Cas saw the items she started crawling away. He crawled after her, growling like an animal, ready to pounce. Cas giggled, smiling behind her pacifier. He chased her back to where the diaper sat and grabbed at her.

"She's gonna bolt if you don't block her. So, you better position her between your legs."

He stretched out his legs in front of him and laid a wiggling Cas down between his knees. "Like this?"

"Yep. Better go fast or she'll get away then you'll have a nudist on the loose." After a few failures and a few muttered cuss words, he finally managed to get it right.

He grinned up at me, holding Cas in his arm. "That wasn't so bad, was it Cas? Course, I'd rather skin a deer than wipe that tar off your hind end, but it's a far cry better than smellin' ya."

"There's a candle on that end table you can light, if you want." I motioned in that direction.

He nodded then locked his gaze with me. "How ya feelin'?"

I studied his eyes, trying to figure out his intentions before responding. He seemed genuinely interested and had at least some concern for me. Maybe I could play nice—for a little while. "I think that bath we had helped. I'm on the mend."

"Can I get you water? Dinner will be ready in about twenty minutes."

"Why are you doin' this?" I asked, narrowing my eyes.

He put Cas back down, sat on his hands and knees to get closer to me. "Because you needed someone to help you." He moved closer like he would kiss my cheek, but I jerked back and put my hand up to block him.

"Don't worry about me getting sick. I have an immune system like an ox." He chuckled and stood up.

"That's not why I didn't want you to kiss me," I shot at him.

A flicker of hurt crossed his features before he walked out of view. He returned with a glass of water and placed it beside me. I know I should have said thank you, but I didn't want to give him that satisfaction. He picked up a fussy Cas and walked with her to look out the sliding door, mumbling something about horses. He took her outside to look at the birds fluttering in the trees, then walked from my view.

I argued with myself, wanting to chase after them, but I was too tired.

He reappeared a few minutes later, laughing. The front of his shirt and shorts dripped water with each step. Cas was soaked, too. I sat taller and scowled. He shook his head. "Don't look so worried. She was just having fun splashing me from the spa." He walked into the kitchen, whispering to Cas as he did, then returned to place her with me. "I better change my shirt."

My eyes widened when he took his shirt off. I sucked in a breath, remembering what it was like to touch those muscles along his torso. Also, remembering what it felt like to be pressed against him, kissing him. My heart rate went double time, and I couldn't keep my eyes off him.

He noticed me watching and winked with a grin on his face. I snapped my head away, pressing my lips together. *Arrogant ... do good ... two faced ... hunky...*

Preston

The sounds of crying woke me, and it took a second or two to get my bearings. *Oh, yeah. I'm at Billie's house and Cas is crying.* I swung my arm over to check the time on my phone and noticed there were more texts from Josie. The clock read three twenty-five. I rubbed my hand down my face and got up to use the toilet. When I finished Cas was still crying, so I headed toward her room.

In the dim of the night light, Billie held Cas to her and paced, singing softly in her ear. She stopped abruptly when she noticed me. *Dang, she looked good in her silk shorts pajamas.* "What are you doing up?" she asked.

Cas lifted her head to me and my heart tugged toward her. "I heard her cryin' and wondered if I could help." I held my hands out to Cas, and she leaned toward me. I grinned, loving that this little jellybean wanted to come to me. I took her in my arms, and she rubbed her head back and forth against my shoulder.

"She's teething. So, she's grumpy and hurtin'," Billie said and immediately folded her arms over her chest. I could tell she wasn't wearing a bra, so I turned my eyes away from her to keep her comfortable with me.

"Is there anything I can do?" I asked.

"Um..."

"You name it, I'll do it."

She sighed then started coughing. When she finished, she spoke, "Well, I don't have any numbing gel for her gums, which would help her a bunch with the discomfort."

Numbing gel? What the crap was that? "Would you like me to go get some? There's a twenty-four hour pharmacy down the road."

"Would you?" She sounded so relieved I decided then and there I always wanted to please her.

"Of course," I answered. "But I have no idea what I'm lookin' for."

"Maybe we could all go. The car ride might help her sleep, and I can help you find the right stuff."

"Sounds good to me, but you should probably put somethin' more on than that, or you'll draw a crowd."

She gave me a look that could kill and walked out of the room. She reappeared, dressed in yoga pants and t-shirt and holding a t-shirt in her hand. "I found one of your t-shirts in your closet, because if you walked around without one, you'd be drawing a crowd."

I grinned. "Is that a compliment?"

She didn't respond. Instead, she took Cas from me and loaded her up in her car seat, which, of course, set her off in a screaming fit. Billie tried to console her, and we made our way out of the house into the SUV. I drove us out of the driveway but paused when I noticed someone standing off to the side of a car at the end of the driveway. They waved, so I stopped once I passed the gate.

"That's a reporter," Billie said and shifted away from her window in the rear seat.

"She looks like she's waving for help." I rolled down my

window.

"Hi. Sorry to bother you, but I've been stuck with a bum starter." She leaned down and glanced in the backseat at the crying baby. "My boyfriend was supposed to come rescue me, but I think he got sidetracked by the bar and is probably drunk off his rocker somewhere," she said between her teeth.

"Do you need a ride home?" I asked. Whether she was a reporter or not she was in need, and I didn't want to turn her away.

"Yes. I'm so tired I could sleep standing up," she responded.

"Get in the front seat," I said, then unlocked the door. She hopped in and took in her surroundings with interest.

"You're a reporter, aren't you?" Billie asked. Leave it to her to get right to the point. Billie coughed a bit, but it honestly was starting to sound better.

"I am. Where y'all headin'?" she asked, smiling.

"My baby is teething so we're just going to get medication to help her."

"In the middle of the night?" she asked.

"Yeah," I answered. "Babies don't typically schedule time for such things at a decent hour."

Billie continued to try to calm Cas during our drive. By the time we reached the store she was livid, and no one could calm her. I twisted in my seat to look at Billie. "You're too sick and weak to go in. I'll go and video call you so you can show me what to get."

She nodded and I hurried in, hoping it was safe to leave the reporter woman with my wife and daughter. *Wait. Wife and daughter.* Those two words warmed me to the core. *I like the sound of that. I wish it could stay that way.*

Finding the right aisle took longer than I'd like to admit. Once I did, I called Billie and showed her in the video what I was looking at. With the correct item in hand, I hurried to the checkout. The process would have gone faster if the cashier hadn't been hitting on me.

When I entered the car, Cas's screams pierced my ears. I held the bag out to Billie. As she worked to soothe her daughter I drove toward the freeway. As Cas's crying eased so did our tension in our shoulders.

"That was the first time I've ever experienced that," the report stated, now able to talk and be heard.

"What's your name?" I asked.

"Jenessa. I already know who you are. Is this a normal occurrence?" She gestured behind her.

"No," Billie said. "Most days it's wonderful. This is a rarity."

"And have you been sick?" Jenessa asked Billie.

"Yes. But getting better," Billie answered.

I glanced at her in the mirror. "And she did ask me to leave, but only because she didn't want me to get sick. Didn't you, darlin'?"

Billie narrowed her eyes only slightly before answering. "Yep. I was worried your entire team would get sick. But he's back to help now that I'm not contagious. And he's been a big help. He even made me chicken soup."

"How domestic," Jenessa responded.

"She's completely asleep, Preston," Billie said with a sigh.

"Turn here," Jenessa said and pointed ahead. "So, there's a rumor that your marriage was a set up. Any comments on that?"

I chuckled. "You know, I fell in love with Billie the first time I met her." *Whoa. Hang on.* I sort of felt the truth of that as I spoke the words. "It's been hard on us that people think we're faking when we love each other so much."

"It's probably just hard for people to believe that couples could fall in love so easily that they have to tear people down," Billie said, neither admitting nor denying whether she loved me back. If she did, she might even be lying anyway.

"So, there really isn't a story here?" Jenessa asked.

"We're just two newlyweds trying to start our family while everyone is watchin'. Can't say it's been easy. I can't even take Cas out for walks anymore," Billie said with venom in her voice, which started a coughing fit.

"I can understand the difficulty. Perhaps I can help by writing something to get everyone off your backs." Jenessa held up a recorder. "I've got what I need to help you out with that. Oh—I live down that street back there. Sorry. Wasn't paying attention."

I did a U-turn. "So, you won't twist our words?" I asked.

"No. You'll get the truth from me. That house right there." She pointed and I pulled to a stop. "Thanks for the ride and to repay you I'll write y'all in a good light."

"Thanks," I felt a little bit better. We said a quick farewell then Billie joined me in the front seat. After we pulled away, I let out a breath I didn't know I was holding. "This has been an odd night."

"What do you think? Will she keep her promise?" Billie asked.

"I hope so."

She held up her phone. "If she tries to bend our words, I also have a recording to prove otherwise."

I laughed and took her hand in mine, kissing the back of it. "You're brilliant, darlin'." I had expected her to pull her hand away and glare, but she surprised me by simply turning to look out of the window and allowing me to hold her hand all the way home.

"So, there's an event comin' up," I said after we drove thirty minutes back home.

"What event?" Billie asked barely above a whisper.

"There's a little shin dig for all the players and their dates this comin' Friday."

"That's only...." she looked at the clock, "a little over a day-ish away. You probably should have told me this sooner," Billie stated.

"Think you'll be better by then?"

"Whether we are or not you'll be expected to go and I'll be expected to be at your arm. Right?"

"Yes. It's a black-tie event."

"Then I guess I better get myself a dress to wear?"

"That would be wise. You'd cause too much of a disruption if you arrived in your birthday suit."

"And you *had* to go and make it weird."

Eighteen

Billie

"A long marriage is two people trying to dance a duet and two solos at the same time." —Anne Taylor Fleming

Something I'd learned over the last eleven months and a few weeks happened to be something that millions upon millions of parents already knew. There was no rest for a mother—even if you're sick. Thankfully, after a long nap, and with the help of a lot of herbal tea and vitamins, I had started to feel nearly one hundred percent.

The morning flew by with me still staying home to recuperate from the virus. Of course, Cas was teething and being a grump. During her naps, I focused on getting work done and called in a cleaning service to erase the events of the last few days and things Preston hadn't cleaned. My parents were due back the following day, just in time to babysit for the black-tie event. Tonight, it was just me and Cas to relax and regenerate.

At least it was just me and Cas until Preston arrived home early in the afternoon.

Annoyingly, his smile greeted me at the door. "Hello, darlin'." He kissed me on the cheek before I could dodge him. He might have been an angel the night before by rescuing us, but that didn't mean he'd changed his mind about me and Cas. He was still in my black book. He picked up Cas from off the floor next to me and spun around with her in his arms. "Hello, Cas!"

Cas started to pout.

"I finally got her to stop crying and you come along and upset her." I stood and took my daughter from his arms.

"Why is she upset?" he asked.

"There's never a clear-cut answer with babies—especially when they're teething. She's just grumpy and uncomfortable."

He stepped closer, rubbing Cas's back and cooing at her. Hearing him talk like a baby pulled at my heart, wishing this was the real him. "What can I do to help her be happy?"

"She just needs time," I said and kissed Cas's cheek. The intercom buzzed, indicating someone was at the gate who wanted to speak to us. I ignored it and went back into my room to fold clothes with Cas.

It buzzed again. "Do you want me to answer that?" Preston called.

"I don't care," I called back to him. "It's probably reporters. Sometimes, they get bold and ring it to see if I'll answer their dumb questions."

A couple of minutes later, the doorbell rang. *What the crap?* I scooped Cas up and hurried to the front entry. Preston had his hand out, ready to open the door. "Wait! Did you let someone in?"

"You have a delivery. So, I let him in." He swung the door open, and there stood a man dressed in the brown uniform and a long box at his side, resting on a handcart. We signed the form on his clipboard, and he wheeled the heavy-looking box into the entry.

Preston ensured the delivery guy had removed himself from the premises, then helped me position the box for opening. He retrieved a pocketknife from his pocket and lowered himself to sit on the floor. He sliced through the tape and opened the box.

I grinned. "My rugs!"

"Wow. That was fast," Preston said. "You bought these in Tunisia, right?"

"Yeah." I set Cas down and started pulling on the first rug to remove it. "I paid extra to ship them faster."

"Here, darlin'. Let me help." Preston lifted the rug up and, with his hands, broke the plastic that held it bound in a roll. He stepped back several steps to give himself room, then flicked his arms to let the rug unroll.

I gasped. "Oh! I'm so glad I went with this color. I love it in here."

A shriek shattered the calm of the room, quickly followed by wailing. I spun around to find Cas on the floor, her fingers spread wide, blood dripping down onto the ground. My lungs seized, and my mind went fuzzy. Preston rushed to Cas and scooped her up, along with the knife he must have left on the floor. "No, no, no, no! Oh, Cas! I'm so sorry!" He ran with her into the kitchen.

Come on, Billie. Snap out of it. It's just blood. Your baby needs you. My legs and lungs heard the call to action, but my head still felt fuzzy on my way into the kitchen. Preston held her hand over the sink with the water running over her fingers.

"Oh, baby girl. I'm so sorry. Shhhh. I'll make it all better, darling," he said over and over. He set her down on the counter, grabbed a paper towel and dabbed at her hand.

The room tilted, so I grabbed hold of the island counter to keep vertical. "Is she…" My mouth didn't want to work, and my voice was so small. "Is she okay?"

He didn't look up but studied the wound instead. "It doesn't look deep enough for stitches."

I lowered my head to rest on the cool granite counter.

"Billie, are you okay?"

"I don't do well with blood," I whispered.

"Go sit down. I'll take care of this."

"No! She's my baby!" I said through clenched teeth. Cas's cries increased in volume.

"And what does that have to do with anything? You think I don't care about her just because she's not mine?" His voice cracked with emotion. "I love her, too! Now, where do you keep the first aid kit?"

I love her, too. Too? What? Did he mean that? Was it *too* like, you love her, and I love her? Or was it, I love her, and I love you, too? By his set jaw and the determined look in his eye, it felt like he spoke the truth. He did love her. It took a second to answer, as I was stunned. "Um. Let me get it."

Now that Preston held Cas's hand in the paper towel and there was no more blood visible, I could function a bit better. I hurried into the bathroom and found the first aid kit easily. When I returned, I placed it on the counter beside him and held my hand out to take Cas.

"I don't want you holding her while standing. In case you faint. Sit down and I'll bring her to you."

I obeyed, sat at the dining chair, and opened my arms to take my baby. I kissed her head and held her tight, while keeping her hand out for him to tend to. As Preston cleaned and bandaged Cas's three little fingers I watched his face. Every few seconds his lips would press tight and his brow would furrow, as if he was inwardly cursing himself.

As he placed the last bandage on her finger I decided to speak up. I couldn't not say anything anymore. I wanted to chew him out. "You said that you love her. How can you be so contradictory?"

His head jerked back in confusion. "What do you mean? Have

I given you a reason to think I don't adore her?"

"Yeah! You said so!" Cas had buried her head into my chest, so when I cried out, she jumped and whimpered more. I kissed her head and apologized.

"When? Why would I have said something like that?"

"On the plane! You said Cassidy is ruining your life!"

He appeared momentarily confused, but then his expression shifted, as if a light had turned on and his memory had returned.

I pointed at him and tried to keep from yelling again, because it was upsetting Cas. "See. You remember saying it, don't you?"

He sighed and shook his head. He stood, pulled out his phone, tapped on it for a second, then held it out to me. "This text…" he swiped, showing me another text, "and this text, and dozens more just like it, are from my ex-girlfriend named Cassidee. Every text is from a different phone number, so I haven't been successful at blocking her completely. What you heard was me talking to one of my friends about how crazy she is and how she doesn't get the hint that we're over."

I took the phone from him, scrolling through screenshots of his short conversations with her.

Hey sexy! This is Cassidee! I've missed you, and I know you're mad at me, but I really, really want to make things right. Please, baby. What we had was right. We were meant for each other…

I skipped down and read his response.

It's over, Cassidee. I'm happily married. Please stop calling and texting.

Text after text of nearly the same pleading and the same response. The dates on the first ones were from before we met on the cruise, but he didn't use the excuse that he was married, simply that he didn't want to get back with her. One of the texts made me believe that she had cheated on Preston.

I handed the phone back to him. "Well, now I feel like an idiot."

He lowered himself to a squat in front of me. He took my hand and looked me in the eyes. "Billie, from the moment I met Cassidy—" he brushed Cas's tears from her cheek, "—*this* Cassidy. *Your* Cassidy—I adored her and fell in love with her. I know it might not seem like it because, honestly, I think I'd suck at this whole dad thing—I mean, look what I did…" His voice broke, and he dropped his head down so I could only see the top of it. His shoulders shook for a moment. When he raised his head, tears spilled from his eyes, and his mouth twisted into an ugly kind of cry. "I've hurt your baby." He covered his lips with his fist. "I'm so sorry for hurting your baby. I didn't even think about the knife on the floor—"

His words were cut off by the force of me pulling him into a one-armed hug.

"I'm so sorry, Billie," he cried into my hair. "I feel like such an idiot."

"You love her?" I asked, hope burning in my chest, thinking of what this could mean. "You love my baby?"

He leaned away enough to see me. "Yes. And I love her mama. Though I don't deserve her or you."

My head jerked back in surprise. What did he just say? I felt the tears burn my eyes as the waterworks turned on. "What?"

He lowered his head again, and I watched his Adam's apple bob up and down. "I'm sorry for hurting you and for causing injury to Cas." He gathered up the bandage garbage and headed out of the room to the hall. The finality of the conversation ended with the shut of his door.

Preston

Smells of some kind of Italian food drifted through the edges of the door, enticing me to leave "my" room. Yet, I couldn't. Partly because I was in the middle of going over our plays for our upcoming games and I needed to get through them one more time to feel like I've improved much. Keeping my mind focused on where it should be proved difficult. Instead, it wanted to replay Cas's face contorting into pain and shock with her hand dripping with blood. Then it would switch to the angry expression on Billie's face as she looked at me, the idiot who left the knife on the floor.

The sun had set, plunging my room into darkness. The only light came from my tablet, the clock, and the salt lamp Billie had left on. I weighed the decision of getting up to turn on the overhead light or just leaving things as they were. A knock at my door startled me. "Yeah?"

"Preston, could you give me a hand for a minute?" Billie asked through the closed door. I could also hear Cas's jabbering and grunts.

She was asking me to help?

Hope surged in my heart before it ceased again with doubts. *What if I screwed things up again?*

"Sure." I closed the cover on my tablet, crossed the room, and opened the door, unsure if I would find an angry Billie, or … who knows.

Her tentative smile caused me to step back. What did that smile mean? Was she still upset and just trying to keep the peace? "Would you mind holding Cas while I finish making dinner? She doesn't want me to put her down."

My arms ached to hold her, but I was apprehensive about touching the fragile darling. "How about I finish dinner and you hold Cas."

"Oh. Okay. I guess dinner isn't too hard." She stepped away and started for the kitchen while I followed.

She gave a few instructions, and I finished chopping veggies for the salad and sauteing the onions and zucchini for the pasta sauce. I finished and plated her a portion, then gave myself a large portion worthy of all football players.

I held up my plate and nodded toward "my" room. "I think I'll take my meal in there, if you don't mind. I need to work on memorizing plays."

"Oh. Um ... actually, I don't like food in the bedrooms." She lowered Cas into a highchair where bits of cooked food waited for her to chuck on the floor. "But you're welcome to eat in the formal dining room. We'll keep quiet in here so we don't disturb you."

"Oh. That will work. Thanks." I took my plate of pasta and salad into the dining room and then retrieved my tablet. While I ate, I listened to the whispers of Billie talking to Cas and her squeaks and yelps in answer. With each passing moment, I wished I could join them, but didn't risk intruding again and think I was part of this family.

After I finished, I helped load the dishwasher and wash a pot. I didn't know where she put everything, so I left the pot I'd cleaned on the counter. While I wiped down the stove, Billie snuck up behind me and startled me by speaking.

"Preston ... I owe you an apology."

"No, you don't," I said, not daring to look at her.

"Yes, I do. I assumed something I shouldn't have and I'm sorry."

"How could you have known otherwise? You didn't know I had an ex with the same name. You have nothing to apologize for." I stepped around her to rinse the cloth in the sink.

"Preston, please. Will you look at me?"

I took a deep breath and turned. Why did she have to be so perfect? Seeing her made me feel even lower. I couldn't look at her for longer than a second. Instead, I watched her fingers rub against her arm.

"I was rude. And cruel. And I hurt you and I'm sorry." Her chin trembled like she was about to cry. "Will you forgive me?"

"There's nothing to forgive."

"Then why won't you look at me?"

Because I'm a fool who doesn't deserve you. Because I've hurt your baby and don't dare touch either of you again. I didn't say either of those things. It wasn't until she sniffed and lifted her hand to wipe her eyes that I looked at her.

Oh, crap. I'm making her cry again. "I can't do anything right by you." My voice shook. "I've hurt your baby, Billie. If it weren't for the stupid reporters, I'd already be gone out of your hair and you'd never have to see me again."

In an instant, she closed the distance between us and wrapped her arms around my torso. It took me a few seconds to respond. I didn't feel worthy of her embrace, but I couldn't push her away and make things worse. I placed my hands at her back and rested my cheek at the side of her head. She felt so good there, but I knew this wouldn't last. I'd screw up somehow and she'd never want to speak to me again.

"A long, long time ago, there was a couple who had an energetic child that liked to jump on beds. They lived in a tiny house where there wasn't much room to walk around the beds, so when they had to iron their clothes, the ironing board sat close to the bed. One morning, while the mom sat on the bed with the bouncing toddler, the dad ironed his clothes before work."

I held my breath, wondering where she was going with this story.

"The mom playfully grabbed at the baby but caused her to fall off the bed instead of moving forward into the safety of the bed. The little girl fell, knocking the hot iron off the board. It landed between the baby's legs, burning her inner thighs. Thankfully, the diaper saved her from worse burns."

I sucked in a breath, thinking of how painful that would be.

"The baby was okay after she healed, of course." She stepped back and looked up at me, keeping me in her arms. "Do you think they should have given up on the idea of caring and loving that daughter because of what they'd done?"

"No."

"Do you think those parents deserved never to love or be loved by that child?"

I didn't answer, though I knew the truth.

"What about a parent driving a car at the time of an accident? Do you think that parent doesn't deserve love because their child was hurt?"

I stepped away, and her arms dropped to her side. "I get where you're going with this, but seeing her hurt by my stupid choice…" *It killed me.*

"I get it. Not even a month ago, I turned the corner into her room with her in my arms and miscalculated, and she hit her head on the doorframe. I felt terrible. Like the worst parent ever." She paused, taking my hand in hers. "Do you think I'm the worst parent ever?"

I huffed and grinned. "That's laughable. You're so far from it. You're a great mama. Anyone can see that."

A soft smile pulled at her lips and her fingers entwined in mine. "You know. I've watched you with Cas, and I think you're gonna be a great dad."

Wait. What did that mean? Did she mean I'd be a great dad in general? Or a great dad to Cas? Do I dare voice that question? Earlier, when I told her I loved her, she didn't respond positively. Her grimace showed me she didn't reciprocate those feelings. I shouldn't have bore my soul. I should have kept my big mouth shut.

She brushed something on my shoulder and then ran her hand down my arm. My heart squeezed, wishing I could deserve her. "Hey," she moved so her face was in line with mine, "how about you help me give Cas a bath and put her to bed? Then later we'll have a bowl of ice cream, and I'll kick your butt in Mario Kart."

I couldn't help the smile that tugged at my lips. "You mean I'll kick your butt in Mario Kart."

She scoffed and walked over to the highchair where Cas was now calling out baby curses at us for ignoring her. "You can keep thinking that, but your dreams of superiority are about to become shattered."

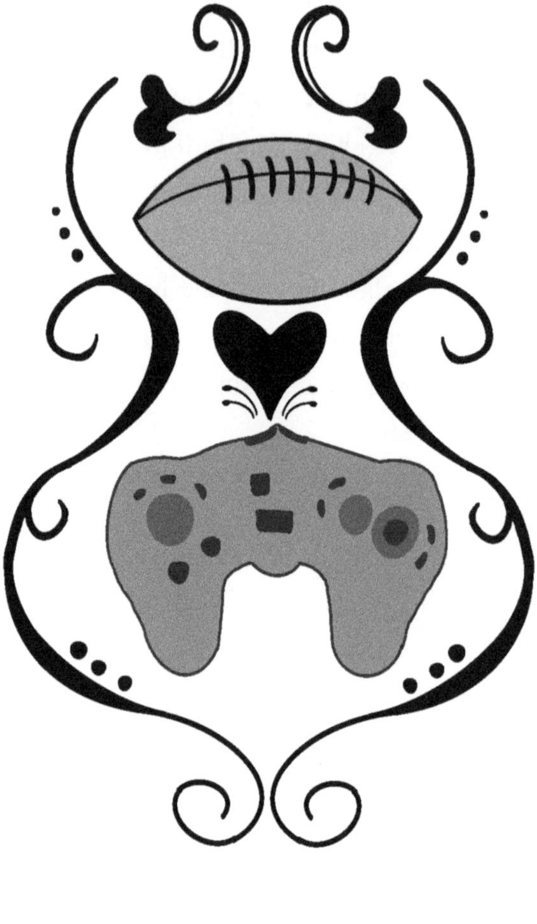

Nineteen

Billie

What do Americans do after winning the World Cup?
Turn off the PlayStation.

Preston made a grave error in his choice of seating. Apparently, he liked sitting on the floor instead of the couch, but he made the mistake of sitting between my knees below me. On the last lap of Bower's Castle, I tucked my foot up between his arm and his abs and flexed my foot so his arm wiggled.

"Oh, you're gonna play like that, huh?" He clamped his arm down, pinning my foot to his side. I laughed and tried to kick free while keeping my first place-spot on the racecourse. My weak, noodle legs were no match for his giant arms. Giggling, I kicked again and again. He paused the game and went full force, tickling my foot.

I screamed and laughed, fully aware that I was no match for his strength, so I fought back in the only way I knew how. I tickled under his arms, but the brute didn't budge or relent. "All right! I give! I give!"

He stopped tickling. "And you'll play fair?"

Oh, my good golly, I loved this playful side. I didn't know if I could coax him out of his funk. I wanted to show him he was no longer in my black book. I felt terrible I'd held so much over his head, ready to light a match and watch him burn. I needed to make it up to him. "Yeah."

"That didn't sound too convincing." He wiggled his fingers a few inches away from my foot.

"I'll play fair," I said, sounding like a car trying to start as I talked between laughing. "But you're taking the fun out of it."

"So, you're good if I cheat, too? Cuz, *girl*, we can go down that road if you're willing to face the consequences."

I leaned forward and whispered in his ear. "Bring it on."

He let go of my foot, stood, and plopped beside me on the couch. "I'm evening the playing field. I was at a disadvantage sitting in front of you." He set his controller aside. "Hang on. I have to eat the rest of my ice cream."

"You waited too long. It's only soup left," I said, then chuckled when he started to slurp it up by tipping the bowl to his mouth. He shifted his eyes only and winked when he saw me watching. His over-exaggerated slurps could wake the neighbors. When he finished, he had a large, thick mustache of cookies and cream milk above his upper lip.

"Uh," I wiggled my finger over my lips to indicate the mess he'd become, "ya gotta little bit of—ah!"

He dove at me, puckering up with his sticky lips. I shoved at his shoulders and his face, trying to keep the goo to himself. His strong arms wrapped around me, crushing against the armrest. I screamed and laughed when his lips touched over my collarbone. A tidal wave of hunger crashed over my body, causing me to gasp and no longer push him away.

He brushed his lips up to my neck and chuckled. "Got you."

My chest rose and fell rapidly, and I couldn't respond.

Next, his tongue moved along the same spot, ending with a few kisses. I closed my eyes, letting the sensation envelop me. *Holy mackerel. So hot!* That is, until I heard Cas cry over the baby monitor. I groaned. "I think I woke her up from my screaming."

"I'll get her," Preston said and sat up, letting me go.

"Hold on. When she wakes up and doesn't need anything, I don't pick her up. I just put my hand on her back and sing to her so she knows I'm there."

"Wow." He tugged me to my feet. "You have that much discipline? I don't think I could stand not holding her when she's crying."

"I know. It was hard at first, but it's better than her crying all the time and wanting to be held all night." Preston followed me in and watched me brush her hair with my fingers as I sang. She simmered down and laid back down by her own choice, falling back to sleep after only a few minutes.

We both exited on tiptoe and returned to the game room. Preston slid his phone from his pocket. "Wow. We've been playing for four hours."

My head jerked back. "Really?"

"I've got practice early, so I should hit the hay." He picked up both our bowls and headed to the kitchen. I followed, turning off all the lights. "Are you going to work in the morning?"

"Yeah. I know it's Friday and I've already missed most of the week, but I need to go over some reports and check in with my team leaders. Plus, it's Larry's birthday and they're having cake in the breakroom."

"When do you leave?" He rinsed the bowl. *He rinsed the bowl! Are you freaking kidding me? Maybe I really do need him around.*

"Around seven. You?"

"Same."

An idea struck, but I wasn't sure how well it would be received, but I voiced it anyway. "Hey, maybe we can carpool. I'm taking Cas with me to work, so I won't have to wait for any sitters."

"Yeah." A smile grew and his eyes lit up. "That will work."

Yay! He liked the idea! "Great." I headed over to the sliding glass door in the family room to lock it. "Oh. I forgot to tell you. My assistant is gonna pick you up a new phone with a new number, so you won't get harassed anymore."

He gave me a look of annoyance. "I don't need a new phone, and even if I did, I can pay for my own."

I shrugged. "It's just a phone. Speaking of being harassed by old girlfriends, how long were you two together?"

He lifted one shoulder to his ear. "A little over a month. Not long enough to get serious, and it ended when she slept with her old boyfriend."

"Ouch. I'm sorry." The only light still on was the light in the entry, which I kept on, and the one in the hall to where we stood.

"I'm not. Not anymore, anyway. I dodged a bullet with that one." He smiled and stepped closer. "Besides, I got lucky with you. If you were smart, *you'd* dodge *me*."

I stepped closer and ran my hand up his chest. "But I'm terrible at playing dodgeball."

"Oh?" He lowered his head, so the side of his nose rested against mine.

I nodded slightly, then brushed my lips over his.

He responded instantly, pulled me into him, instigating a dance between our lips. His kisses were slow and deliberate, as if he wanted the moment to last forever. My body shivered with desire, but I knew there was a line I could not cross. I still didn't know where this relationship was heading. What if we found out we weren't compatible? What if he grew tired of me?

I gently pushed away but kissed him a couple more times so he didn't feel complete rejection. "I better get to bed."

"Billie ... I..." He sighed, then nodded. "Yeah. Goodnight, darlin'." He kissed my forehead and then stepped back to his door. "See you in the morning."

It took ages to finally go to sleep. I kept thinking of him across the hall, wishing he wasn't.

Preston

Leaving early in the morning for practice had always been a breeze; I could just get up and go. Not today, though. Today I had two people tagging along, slowing me down. But the funny thing was, I loved every second of it. We even devised a better plan by having Billie drop me off since having Cas with her would make it easier with the stroller and backpack and all. A month ago, I hadn't a clue how much stuff a baby needed to go anywhere. Crazy but necessary.

Billie dropped me off with the promise of returning at two. I'd be finished long before then, but I figured I could spend a little time with Coach going over some plays.

As I was changing in the locker room I received a text. Figuring it was Billie, I hurried to respond. It wasn't Billie. It was Josie.

Hey lover boy! I know this little game you're playing with Billie isn't real and you're wishing you'd snagged me instead. So, I'm giving you another chance. Meet with me. Give me one night or your little fake dreamworld will come crumbling down.

I sighed heavily, dropping my head back against the locker. Why can't women be reasonable and not psycho?

Josie. I've tried to be kind and spare your feelings but now with you threatening me you've crossed the line. It's not gonna happen. Billie and I are real, so let it go and get a life.

I burned the frustrations of both her and Cassidee's texts out on the field, followed by our warmups. Three-fourths of the way through, Delany nudged me with his padded shoulder and pointed with his chin into the stands nearby. "Hey, I see a redhead with an adorable baby on her lap."

My head jerked around to see where he pointed. My heart leapt, seeing her bright smile. I lifted a hand and waved. Billie's waving hand felt like a hundred perfect throws over the endzone. She lifted Cas up and helped her wave, too.

I jogged over until I reached the wall near her seat. "Look. There's Daddy. Wave to Daddy," Billie said to Cas as she stood and met me at the barrier wall.

Emotion caught in my throat. *Daddy. She just referred to me as Daddy.* When I thought I couldn't feel more overjoyed, Cas waved. Her chubby little hand flapped about as her arm pumped up and down.

Billie gasped. "She waved! Preston! She waved. On her own!"

"That's my girl," I said, hoping my voice wouldn't catch and my tears would stay inside. I climbed the side, reached over the rail, and brushed my fingers on Billie's cheek. "You're here."

"We decided work was too boring, so we left. Besides, I wanted a chance to see you in your getup." Billie leaned forward and wiggled her brows up and down. "You look smokin' hot in those tight pants."

That's it. I'm done for. My heart will never be the same after that look she gave me. I stood on my toes to reach her, placed my hand behind her head, and kissed her. I felt her tug at the neck of my jersey, pulling me in closer. She tilted her head, taking the kiss further. At that very second, I hated the shoulder pads, this wall—everything that kept me from her. I wanted her in my arms, never to leave again.

Cas squawked in our ears, bringing us back to earth.

I stepped back, feeling dazed. "I'm glad you came." I couldn't help my stupid grin, and I knew the guys were gonna tease me relentlessly, but I didn't care. I was in love.

Billie held up a small box. "I got you a new phone. I already charged it for you and programmed my number in. It's under, Goddess of Gaming, Winner of Mario Kart."

I rolled my eyes. "Did all of that really fit in the name line?"

"No. But I wish it had."

I laughed and kissed her again. "Hold onto the phone and meet me outside the locker room when we're finished."

"Yes, sir. Break a leg."

"That's not something you say to a football player, darlin'."

"Oh. Bust some skulls then." She waved at me and spoke to Cas once again. "Wave to daddy."

If this were a game, I'd be soaring so high, no one would be able to stop me.

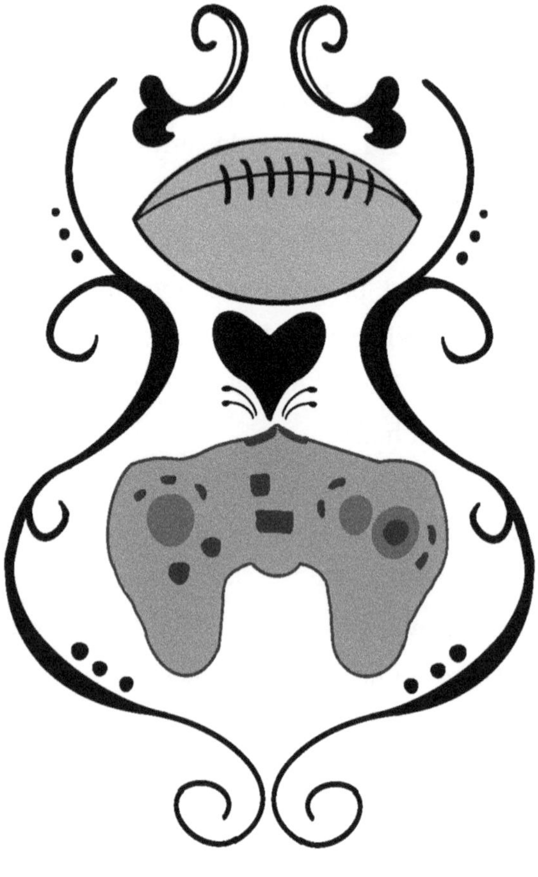

Twenty

Billie

"A successful marriage requires falling in love many times, and always with the same person."
—Mignon McLaughlin.

The look on Preston's face when I exited my room with my evening gown on for the black-tie event gave me nervous anticipation that vibrated in my limbs. I fidgeted with everything I touched. He liked my off-the-shoulder gown. I knew because he repeatedly told me how beautiful I was both at home and on the drive over, and his eyes drifted over my neck and shoulders often.

He rocked the tux, but I still couldn't forget the image of his butt in his football uniform.

Earlier in the day, I sent my jet to pick up my parents to be one hundred percent sure they'd make it home to babysit for me. So, I arrived at the shindig on a high note with my baby being cared for by the best people. My dress looked fantastic and my man at my side couldn't take his eyes off me.

The grand ballroom at the hotel was over the top, beautiful in decoration, mixing elegant with the whole sportsy football stuff. Add to that, all the people milling about in tuxedos and gowns, it set a tone of elegance. When we first arrived, we were met by Koa and Delany and their dates, who I'd bet my signed set of Tolkien books were models.

"Hey, it's the newlyweds!" Koa laughed. He gave me a hug and spoke in my ear loud enough he could be heard over the music. "Has he been treating you like a queen, Billie?"

I whispered back, "He has."

He stepped away and spoke to both of us. "When are we gonna celebrate the union?"

"Oh," I shot a look at Preston, "I hadn't thought about it." But I did think about it during our conversation as a group. If we did choose to continue this marriage I would want to celebrate with friends and family. Much like we did with Preston's family. I'd like our families to meet. I'd want to show off my man to the ones in my life.

Twenty minutes into the event Noah arrived with Josie on his arm. *Oh, goody*, I groaned internally. Noah instantly started up conversations with a group near the door, but Josie didn't seem interested. I watched as her eyes scanned the room and landed on Preston who stood holding my hand. Greed flashed in her eyes before they drifted to me. Hatred burned from her. She rolled her eyes and turned her back to me, only then taking interest in the group speaking with Noah.

Preston guided me on to meet with some of the coaches and other players. It was odd to have so many people mention my wealth like it was an accomplishment for Preston to have snagged someone with money. It irked me, but I bit my tongue and kept quiet. After the fourth person made such a comment Preston rolled his eyes. "As if that's the reason why we married."

"Yeah. From what I heard you weren't married until after returning home," the half-drunk linebacker said with a laugh.

I stiffened and Preston jerked his head back. "Where did you hear something so stupid as that?"

"It's all over social media." He leaned into me. "When you decide to toss him to the curb, come find me. I've got enough loving to keep you warm at night."

"Excuse me!" I about slapped the man, but we were interrupted by Henry, the PR rep I'd met at one of our meetings.

"Sorry for disturbing y'all, but can I speak with you two?" he asked me and Preston.

Preston took my hand and followed Henry to a quiet corner of the room near a giant poster of the Nighthawks' mascot. "What's up?"

Henry didn't say a word, only handed over a tablet open to a photo of Preston and Josie. Behind them, the Colosseum in Roma. Her hand rested on his chest and her head leaned in toward his. I could tell by how he held his body that one arm rested behind her on the rail. The other rested at his side. She looked cozy. He didn't. But that's not what the comment said.

We both read a report quoting Josie.

"There was nothing indicating that they had a relationship while on the cruise." The reporter quoted Josie. "In fact, Preston and I hooked up while on the cruise, so if they were even married, they sure didn't act like it. It's all fake."

My hand dropped from the tablet that Preston and I had held. I pressed on my stomach, hoping I didn't spew up the glass of champagne and hors d'oeuvres. My eyes locked with Preston's, and my panic must have been evident. Without hesitation, he shoved the tablet back into Henry's hand, took me by the elbow, and guided me around to the other side of the poster, between it and the wall.

"Josie is a conniving liar." His eyes darted between mine, the look in them desperate. "Please tell me you don't believe her."

"I … don't…" I blinked, trying to keep any tears from forming.

"Billie. Jumping from one woman to another isn't me. I wouldn't have shown so much interest in you then moved on to anyone so quickly. That day Josie told me you were a gold digger—which is completely not true. I know that now. I'm sorry I didn't then."

"So, nothing happened between you two?" I asked, my voice breaking.

"Nothing. In fact, she tried to make a move on me several times and I turned her down—she even tried to kiss me—well, she did kiss me, but I didn't kiss her back nor did I encourage it. Please believe me, Billie."

I rubbed my temple, feeling a headache coming on. Thinking back on all the times I'd interacted with Josie I came to the same conclusion he had. Josie was a conniving liar. She'd lied about so many things. One that really bothered me at the time and still did, was her taking credit for the cruise exertion that I made for the guys.

I pursed my lips and locked eyes with Preston. From my expression he must have concluded I didn't believe him. His shoulders sank and his face grew remorseful. "Billie. Please—"

I softened my expression and took his hand. "I do believe you, Preston. And I'm pissed off at what Josie is doing to us."

Hope filled his eyes. "You believe me?"

I stepped closer, running my hands up his chest. "I believe you."

He let out a great puff of air and smiled. He eased me into a hug and whispered in my ear. "Oh, Billie. I love you, and I don't ever want to lose you. Thank you for trusting me."

My heart felt like it had made a touchdown and was celebrating by doing laps. Not that I had ever experienced it, but I could imagine it would feel just as thrilling. "You love me?"

He leaned back so he could see my face. He brushed at my cheek as he held my head under my ear. "I love you, Billie. I was afraid to tell you sooner—well, I sort of did tell you already, but I'll say it again and again…" He rested his forehead on mine. "I love you."

"Does that mean you want to keep me and Cas?" It hurt so much to put my heart out there and ask the question, but his declaration of love gave me hope.

"I know I don't deserve you, but if I can't keep you, I think I'll die. Please, will you let me be a part of your family? Let me be a true husband to you?"

"Are you proposing to me, Preston?" I asked playfully.

"Yes."

"Then my answer is yes, and I'm glad we're on the same level." I sighed, happy to finally release the truth. "And I love you, so much."

His chuckle sounded like a release of pent-up worry. He tugged me in, kissing me first on my lips, then every inch of my face. I threw my arms around him and kissed his lips over and over, each one willed with hope for the future. He picked me up and swung me around as our lips were locked. My leg hit the metal post holding up the poster.

Crash! The poster came down, revealing our hiding spot and us both in lips lock with each other. Everyone in the room pulled out a phone to take pics as we turned our heads, still in our embrace, to gawk back at them.

"Oops," Preston said, then added, "We're newlyweds in love. What do you expect?"

I threw my head back and laughed, then pressed my lips to his once again. People whooped and hollered at us kissing. When someone yelled for us to get a room is when Preston decided to end the blissful experience.

He leaned his head into my ear. "Can we do more of that later?"

"How about you move into my room tonight and see where

more of that takes us," I said with a smile growing and energy zinging through my body.

His eyes grew and he grabbed my arm and started pulling me toward the door. "I think we've stayed long enough."

I laughed and eased him to a stop, kissing his cheek. "Hang on, honey love. I need to talk to your friends first."

I tugged him over to where Delany, Koa and Noah stood with their dates, along with another couple I had yet to meet. Henry followed us over, and I tapped away on my phone, finding the invoice I needed to take care of Josie once and for all. On my way over I tapped Henry on the shoulder and asked him to video what was about to happen.

"Hey guys," I said, stopping beside Noah. "I was just reminiscing with Preston here about our cruise trip and how awesome the excursion was that we went on together."

"That was an awesome excursion," Noah said and leaned into Josie as though she should be adored.

"Yeah. It was cool." I agreed. "And ya remember how I was trying to hide who I was at the time, so I didn't get bombarded with people while on vacay? Well, that was the whole reason I didn't tell you guys that *I* was the one who bought the excursion tickets. I guess I felt so bad you guys would be stuck on the ship while in the most perfect historical place in the world. I just had to do it."

Josie's eyes grew hard, glaring at me.

"Wait." Delany held up his hand. "I thought Josie bought them for us."

"Well, of course that's what she wanted you to think. Professional liars are good at making things up like that, but as you can see," I held up my phone, showing the invoice for the extra tickets, "I did, in fact, purchase them. Crazy, huh?"

Everyone's heads turned to Josie. She stiffened and started to stammer. "Well—I had to—um—"

"So, you lied." Koa folded his arms and sized her up.

"Well, I—"

"She's lied about a ton of things, like her supposed relationship she and I had on the ship," Preston said with a lift of his brow.

"Dude! You were trying to dodge her claws the whole time." Koa laughed and slapped Preston on the shoulder. "There's no way you'd have hooked up with her."

Henry stepped up, holding his phone that recorded the encounter. "So, you've lied about sleeping with Preston?"

Her red face looked like it would pop. "I knew he wanted to. He was totally into me. And it's not like they've been honest about their fake relationship either." She pointed at me.

Preston stepped closer to her, standing with his shoulders back, looking like he'd take her down here and now. "I happen to be head over heels in love with my *wife*. There's nothing fake about that."

"Oh, honey." I yanked Preston back to me and wrapped my arms around him. "I love hearing you say that."

I rubbed his nose with mine and he pressed me against him. "And I'll say it every day if my reward is your smile."

I ran my fingers into his hair. "Oh, you're gettin' more than a smile, Preston."

"You two need to get a room. You're so disgustingly in love." Koa rolled his eyes then rubbed his hand down his face.

"I think that's our cue to leave, darlin'." Preston turned back to the group and pointed at Josie. "You'd best get rid of her, Noah. She's nothing but bad news."

Noah scoffed. "No doubt, she is." He took her by the arm and practically growled at her. "I'll call you a cab. It's time for you to leave."

"And if you try messing with us again, *Josie*," I mocked, "I'll sue you so fast and drag it out so long you won't have two pennies to rub together when I'm finished with you."

With her fists clenched and her eyes so narrow, she blew like Mt Vesuvius. She threw a fit worthy of the women on Bridezilla. Preston and I left, leaving those in the room ample opportunity to take videos to share on social media of her meltdown, which wouldn't last long given that we passed a few security guards racing to the grand ballroom.

We retrieved our car from the valet and headed home, getting honked at each light change because we were a little preoccupied. Yeah. Kissing and driving didn't exactly mix.

We arrived home and found my parents throwing elbows as they played Mario Kart in the game room. Cas had gone to sleep hours before, so my parents were sticking around in the main house to listen for her if needed. But now that we were home, they could scram. Which I hoped they would. And fast.

Dad turned off the game and stood. "You're home early."

"Yeah," Preston removed his tux coat and tossed it over a chair. "We decided a quiet night home with just the two of us would be better."

I slipped my arms around Preston's torso and smiled up at him. "A much better idea, I'd say." Preston smiled down at me then pressed his forehead to mine.

"Oh," Mom said, then her eyes went wide. "Oh! Well, then. I guess we'll leave you to hold down the fort." She grabbed Dad's hand and started yanking him toward the door. "We haven't heard a peep from Cas, so she's all good."

"Thanks, Mom and Dad." As they walked from the room, I gave each one of them a hug and kiss on the cheek.

Mom held me a bit longer and whispered in my ear. "So, what's going on with you and Preston?"

I whispered back. "We love each other, and we want to stay married."

Mom leaned back, grabbed both my hands in hers and squealed with her mouth shut as though trying not to let Preston know how excited she was at the news. He, of course, noticed and chuckled, pulling me from my mom and into his arms.

"Well, we better go. Have a good night, you two." Dad smirked and left with Mom in his arm.

As soon as they were out of sight Preston lifted me into his arms, cradling me to his chest like a new bride. "Well, Mrs. Kyler, I do believe we are alone." He chuckled and carried me down the hall toward my room—*our* room.

"And what are your intentions with me, Mr. Kyler?"

He lowered me beside the bed after shutting the door with his foot. "I plan to make you happy, every possible second I can for the rest of my life." He kissed me, telling me with his tender lips that he cherished me.

I leaned away after a few kisses and gazed into his eyes. "And I plan to do the same, Preston. I want us to be happy, even through our hard times." He kissed me a few more times, then I pushed him away. "Wait. I have a few questions I don't know your opinion on."

"And you want to know now?" he asked, with an eye roll.

I slapped his shoulder playfully. "How long do you want to wait to have kids?"

He grinned. "Who says we have to wait? Having Cas in my life makes me really want more. Even if I really suck at being a dad."

I gave him my best stern look. "You don't suck. And you seriously want kids right away?"

"Heck, yeah. Do you?"

I nodded while biting my lip.

"I'd like to do something for you. Can I do something for you?"

he asked.

I kissed his neck. "Whatever it is, I'm sure it can wait."

His breath trembled as he held me tighter. He growled and chuckled before speaking again. "I would like to give you a wedding. The cake. The flowers. The dress—all of it. Cas can be the flower girl. A big wedding or a small one. Whatever you choose. My wedding gift to you."

My eyes grew as they filled with tears. "Are you serious?"

"Yes." He kissed my nose. "You need your dream wedding."

"I guess better late than never, huh?"

He nodded and leaned his head down, brushing his lips on mine. "I love you, my darling wife."

My heart soared and my body shuttered with anticipation and love. "I love you, my hunky quarterback. Now let's go make some babies."

And we did. Several of them—after we threw a dream wedding to remember the rest of our days.

Sign up for my newsletter to read Ivory's story in a free short story at Authorchristinemwalter.com.

Thank you for reading! I am honored you'd take the time to read what I have to share! I've got loads more coming, so please give this book a review on Goodreads and Amazon. Doing so will help me publish more, and have I got a plethora of stories to share, and between you and me, more than a dozen are already completed—rough drafts still—but completed. AND I've started over two dozen more. So, hold onto your seat, because it's all coming as quickly as they can get edited and time permits.

Yes, most of my stuff so far has been time travel, but I've got some Regency, suspense romances, and romantic comedies—all of which are completed and waiting for editing. If you can't wait to read all of this crazy that's been going on in my head, then follow me on Instagram and Tiktok for updates on what's new, and sign up for my newsletter on my website.

@AuthorChristineMWalter (Instagram)

@AuthorChristineMW (Tiktok)

@ChristineWalterAuthor (Facebook)

Check out **www.authorchristinemwalter.com** to join my newsletter!

Other Books by Christine M. Walter

Shariton Park Series

A Time for Shariton Park

A Season for Shariton Park

Short Stories/Novella Collection

Unexpected Romance Collection

Stand Alone
Heartthrobs and Hauntings

Through Time Series (Six Books)

A Countess Through Time
A Siren Through Time
A Scoundrel Through Time (coming soon)

Acknowledgments

There ain't no way in h-e-double-hocky-sticks I could have published on my own. It takes a village. There are so many people to thank, my head is spinning. There is so much to do and so many people involved in publishing a book, whether the author is self-published or not. To thank everyone sufficiently would be a monumental task of its own, and quite frankly, I could never thank y'all enough. First, I'd like to thank my children and my hunk of sugar lovin' husband for giving me time and support to write.

Thank you to my editors, Alexa and Roxana, for the crap load of junk you had to shift through to polish my work to what it is now. If there are any mistakes, they're all on me. Sometimes I can't see what's right in front of my face, so they are lifesavers. A huge shout out and thanks to Katie Garland at Sapphire Midnight Design for the beautiful cover. Thanks to my family and friends who have encouraged me in getting my stories out there. A great big appreciation to Lynette Taylor, you were the first to push me to write, so thanks for giving me confidence to do so. Traci, thanks for the pat on the back, the kindness, and the inspiration to keep going. Thanks to my Sweet Tooth Critique group for all your feedback. Also my ANWA writer's group. You ladies rock! Thanks to all the Youtubers, book reviewers, and other authors on social media who have shared their publishing stories and advice with the world. It's a huge support to those starting off.

And thank you to my readers!
Here's to dreams and many more stories! Cheers!

About Christine M Walter

Christine adores her husband, her three adult*ish* children, and her attention-seeking dog, Chewbacca, so much that she'll pause writing and reading just for them. Well, most of the time. When she's not drawn to writing, she often spends time in lego building, painting, drawing, hiking, rock collecting, and off-roading through saguaro cactuses near her home in Arizona. Christine's artwork has been featured in the novel *Blackmoore* by Julianne Donaldson, as well as in the movie *8 Stories*. Christine has been the recipient of multiple awards in the first chapter contests and most recently won honorable mention for a first page contest from Gutsy Great Novelist and she won two awards in the ANWA BOB contest. Seeing new places and experiencing new cultures are top on her list of desires. In fact, her sense of adventure inspired her and her family to sell their home, move into a 400-square-foot RV, and travel the country simply to see and enjoy life outside of the norm. Best year ever!

Get to know how weird she is by following her social medias!
@AutherChristineMWalter (Instagram)
@AuthorChristineMW (Tiktok)
@ChristineWalterAuthor (Facebook)
Check out her website at www.authorchristinemwalter.com and sign up for her newsletter for a free short story!